"You F[...]
Good N[...]

"I don't kiss stran[...]
night!" She tossed [...] defiantly.

He took a step forward and suddenly wrapped his arms about her in a rough embrace. "I'm no stranger to you," he said thickly.

"Then why do you always behave as though you are?" she asked, trembling.

"Because you're such a saucy wench!" His white teeth flashed in a wicked smile. Then he kissed her full on the mouth.

Off again, on again, her brain warned her. Then everything dissolved except the force of his body against hers, and the possessive thrust of his lips.

MARY CARROLL

is an internationally known American writer who has published both here and abroad. She brings to her romantic fiction a varied background of teaching and traveling that gives her a unique insight into the world of romance.

Dear Reader:

Silhouette Books is pleased to announce the creation of a new line of contemporary romances—*Silhouette Special Editions*. Each month we'll bring you six new love stories written by the best of today's authors— Janet Dailey, Brooke Hastings, Laura Hardy, Sondra Stanford, Linda Shaw, Patti Beckman, and many others.

Silhouette Special Editions are written with American women in mind; they are for readers who want more: more story, more details and descriptions, more realism, and more *romance*. *Special Editions* are longer than most contemporary romances allowing for a closer look at the relationship between hero and heroine with emphasis on heightened romantic tension and greater sensuous and sensual detail. If you want more from a romance, be sure to look for *Silhouette Special Editions* on sale this February wherever you buy books.

We welcome any suggestions or comments, and I invite you to write us at the address below.

Karen Solem
Editor-in-Chief
Silhouette Books
P.O. Box 769
New York, N. Y. 10019

MARY CARROLL
Take This Love

Silhouette Romance

Published by Silhouette Books New York

America's Publisher of Contemporary Romance

Other Silhouette Books by Mary Carroll

Divide the Wind
Shadow and Sun
Too Swift the Morning

SILHOUETTE BOOKS, a Simon & Schuster Division of
GULF & WESTERN CORPORATION
1230 Avenue of the Americas, New York, N.Y. 10020

ISBN: 0-671-57120-6

First Silhouette Books printing December, 1981

10 9 8 7 6 5 4 3 2 1

America's Publisher of Contemporary Romance

Printed in the U.S.A.

Chapter One

Jamie MacPherson clutched the wheel of her second-hand Austin and strained forward to see the road ahead through the sleet-spattered windshield. Slick and wet, it shot straight up into the clouds—"the Pass of the Cattle" it had once been called by her Gaelic forebears, and she wished now for one of their shaggy Highland beasts in place of the wheezing Austin to carry her safely to Applecross.

For most of her twenty-four years she had dreamed of seeing these wild and windswept Scottish Highlands, but now that she was here, her stomach knotted in terror at the switchbacks that faced her, and the icy rain, streaked with snow, forbade even one comforting glimpse of the dark, lovely glens she knew must lie below.

It was late April, and this day—the twenty-fourth —had been circled in red on her calendar ever since Ian MacPherson, the titular head of the clan Mac-Pherson and laird of Talbert Hall, had written her of Angus MacPherson's death.

Jamie had never known her great-uncle, but on his ninetieth birthday she had penned a note of congratulations to him and inquired about the history of the clan, which had ever fascinated her. Though he had not replied, evidently he had treasured her letter, for it was her address in the letter's right-hand corner that had prompted Ian to inform her of Angus's demise and to say as well that as far as could be ascertained, Jamie MacPherson of 40 Beakbottom Lane, London, was his only heir.

Ian's letter had gone on to explain that the inheritance was meager—a few sticks of furniture and a shelf of books, and the right to renew indefinitely the lease on the croft. The rent was paid up until the following January, and the cottage was available for habitation if the heir so desired.

In wide-eyed disbelief, Jamie had stared at the letter. *The heir most certainly did desire!*

For more than two years the slender, raven-haired young woman had been studying art in the evenings while she plotted an escape from her job as a shop assistant near Trafalgar Square. Six months was what she hoped for, or possibly a year if she could manage it. She had hoarded away a small nest egg, humming all the while, "My heart's in the Highlands," but fearing at the same time that when she did make her break it would carry her no farther from London than the Devon coast.

She wanted to paint the faces that she saw, and the glorious crags and valleys and moors she imagined in Scotland, but she had only the faintest hope of getting there until Ian MacPherson's letter had come, a bolt out of the blue that snapped the economic fetters binding her to London's foggy streets. As soon as she could arrange her affairs, she took the money she had set aside for rent during her hiatus and bought the Austin and set forth.

Now if the blasted machine could be cajoled to

climb this last perpendicular five miles into Apple-cross, life on the Talbert Hall estate would, in a matter of minutes, become a reality!

The Austin, however, had other ideas. Just as it reached the craggy crest—with another equally formidable one appearing ahead—it issued a series of coughs and then stopped altogether. With fierce determination, Jamie struggled with the starter, realizing at the same time she could never make it go again. Five miles remained of the worst road she had seen in her life, and the thing was dead!

Desperate, she opened the car door thinking to have a peep under the bonnet, but a blast of sleet stung her face, and she slammed it shut again. Huddling beneath the steering wheel, she gave herself up to panic. What would happen to her out here all alone? She couldn't even remember the last car that had passed her. Even if one did happen by, it might only slam into the Austin in the blinding sleet.

Imagining such a jolt, she all but jumped out of her skin when there was a sudden pounding on the windowpane at her ear. Then, wild with relief, she realized it was not a crash, but someone who had come to her rescue.

Hastily, she rolled down the glass, and then drew back with equal haste as a thick tangle of black, sleet-encrusted hair covering the head and jaw of a man was thrust into the car. Wide shoulders covered by a shepherd's smock of heavy gray homespun filled up the window, and only the piercing gaze of a pair of blue eyes silenced the yelp of alarm that crowded at Jamie's throat.

"Are you stalled?"

The voice, deep and reassuringly civilized, caused

Jamie to let go a sigh of relief. "I'm afraid so. Do you think you can start me up again?"

With a rumble of laughter, the man withdrew his head. "You don't expect this puny machine to carry you into A' Chomraich, do you?"

Jamie got out of the car, abashed by the rugged, six-foot frame of the man who towered beside her. "It has to. It's all I have."

Her rescuer took a slow turn around the car, eyeing it with the same frank amusement he might have bestowed on a child's toy.

Jamie lifted her delicate chin. "Anyway, I'm not going to—wherever that was you said. I'm on my way to Applecross."

His booming laugh came again. "A' Chomraich is the Gaelic name for Applecross." He gave her the same look he had given the car. "It means 'the Sanctuary.'"

"I could certainly use one of those!" Jamie had suddenly realized she was freezing to death. Sleet had collected in her own black hair and she was trembling from top to toe. "What do you suggest I do?"

In answer, the man put a thick shoulder against the back window of the Austin, and with what seemed for him the slightest shove, he eased it off onto the spongy roadside. "We'll let it sit there overnight. You can send someone back in the morning for it."

A five-mile tow charge? Jamie's shivering increased. Her budget could not accommodate an expense of that nature, but she had a more pressing worry at the moment. "How will I get to Applecross?"

The man lifted dark brows. "With me, of course. How else?"

For the first time Jamie saw his Jeep pulled off on the opposite side of the road. Behind its steamy glass, two black and white sheep dogs, paws perched on the dashboard, lolled their pink tongues at her in a friendly fashion.

"Are you a shepherd?"

The man's piercing blue eyes moved with frank curiosity over her trim body. "You might say that."

"Then why would you be going in to Applecross?"

He saw the flush his appraisal had raised, and the corners of the sensuous mouth that cut a proud, crooked line across his craggy face curled in amusement. "What would I do with you if I didn't?"

Jamie stiffened. "You're kind to go out of your way."

"I can't very well leave you out here to freeze," he answered brusquely and started toward the Jeep. "But hurry along, please. I'm looking for a lamb."

"In this blizzard?" Jamie challenged him. "I can't imagine that there would be lambs about now."

"It's spring," her rescuer answered with unconcealed irritation.

"Well, it certainly doesn't feel like it!"

"Then get inside," he commanded and flung open the door of his vehicle. Immediately, the dogs began to bark, but he silenced them with a curt command and they jumped to the floor and settled there quietly.

Jamie looked back at the Austin. "What about my things?"

"Which ones do you want?"

"All of them, please." If the tow charge was out of

reason, she might have to leave the car beside the road indefinitely. "I can help."

"Stay where you are," he answered, and with a scowl crossed the road again. Three trips were required before he had everything, and the last he completed with her easel swung over his shoulder and her paint box tucked beneath his arm.

When he had crammed everything into the rear of the Jeep, he slid behind the wheel and shot her an openly critical look.

"I'm sorry there were so many things," she said.

"You'd do well to have a caravan," he answered gruffly, and started the motor. In a moment they were hurtling along at a breakneck speed up the slippery road. Then suddenly he veered off to the right into a kind of gully, giving the Jeep such a jolt—and all of its occupants, as well—that the paint box spilled open, and tubes, brushes and jars of acrylic came tumbling out from under the seat, setting the dogs off once again.

"Blast!" He slammed on the brakes. "What's all this?"

"My supplies." Jamie scrambled to the floor. "I think you've ruined half of them."

"You've ruined them yourself, starting out to Applecross in a sardine can. Why didn't you consult a map before you began?"

Jamie cut angry violet eyes at him. "Why don't you go and look for your lamb?"

Folding his arms, he stared straight ahead. "When you get that mess cleaned up."

There was scarcely room in the bottom of the Jeep for Jamie to maneuver, but finally—with no help from either her companion or his dogs—she managed. Red-faced and fuming, she pulled herself up onto the seat. "Anytime you're ready, *sir,*" she said tightly.

"The name," he answered with cold condescension, "is Ian MacPherson."

Jamie barely blinked. "I suppose the hills are full of them. MacPhersons," she said in response to his scowl. "*Ian* MacPhersons, to be exact." In her corner of London alone, seven Henry MacPhersons were listed in the directory, and five Williams.

"There are MacPhersons aplenty here in the west, 'tis true." His proud gaze stayed on her. "But I am the only Ian."

Jamie turned down her rose-tinted lips. "Ian MacPherson is laird of Talbert Hall. You're a shepherd."

"Of course I'm a shepherd." He gave her a scorching glance and started the Jeep. "Of a very large flock, I might add."

"One of which is lost." Annoyed with his air of superiority, she turned her face to the window. If this man were kin to her, she was glad he didn't know it. "Where will you look first?"

They found the lost lamb tangled in the bracken, but not before Jamie had sneezed twice and Ian had brought forth a heavy wool jacket from the back of the Jeep and thrown it across her shoulders. It swallowed her, of course, but after a few minutes wrapped in its welcoming warmth, she forgot how ridiculous she must look trudging along beside the giant of a man to whom it belonged, and she concentrated her attentions on the search.

It was Jamie, in fact, who discovered the lamb. When she saw the pitifully bleating bit of life ensnared in the thicket, the resentment she felt toward Ian vanished.

"Come quick!" she called eagerly, and at once he and the dogs were at her side. In a matter of minutes, Ian's strong, capable hands lifted the lamb to safety, but Jamie insisted on taking it beneath her warm jacket.

"What shall we do with it?" she inquired, trying to keep up with Ian's strides on the way back to the Jeep. "Isn't its mother around here somewhere?"

"Probably, but I haven't time to hunt for her. I'll take the lamb home and come out again in the morning."

Jamie frowned. "I thought a shepherd stayed with his flock."

He gave a curt laugh. "He must gather the flock first, and that is precisely what I intend." His tone smacked of self-satisfaction. "I shall gather my flock —and a very special gathering it promises to be."

He seemed absorbed in his own thoughts after that, and Jamie, absorbed herself with the lamb, said nothing else, either, until the tidy white cottages of Applecross began to appear on the horizon. The sleet had stopped before they had begun to hunt for the lamb, and though the sun remained hidden, a kind of gray glare had settled over the landscape and allowed enough clarity for the full charm of the village to make itself known.

"How lovely!" Jamie breathed.

The town, laid in a large, level glen, was a welcome sight after the perilous peaks the Jeep had scaled, and its white stone cottages arranged in a line along the Sound seemed cozy and inviting to the travel-weary Jamie.

"Where do you want to get out?" demanded Ian.

"I don't know—the hotel, I suppose. Or the constable's office. Anyplace where someone can direct me to Talbert Hall."

Once again the Jeep came to a jolting halt.

"What in blazes, woman!" Ian's blue eyes seemed on fire. "If it's Talbert Hall you want, why did you drag me to Applecross?"

Jamie surveyed him, nostrils flared. Her violet eyes, fringed with sooty lashes, looked at him stormily. "Because Applecross is where Talbert Hall is."

"The devil you say! The estate is seven miles to the east in the direction we've just come from. I told you who I was. Why didn't you say what you wanted?"

"You told me your name was Ian MacPherson. You did *not* say you were laird of Talbert Hall—and even if you had, I wouldn't have believed you."

"Why in thunder not?"

"Because the laird is a gentleman." Jamie's gaze raked his rugged attire. "I have letters from him in my purse that the likes of you could never have written, and I am sure he will not appreciate it when I tell him that one of his clansmen is impersonating him."

Ian turned on her such a look of outraged astonishment that she shrank toward the window. "Besides"—she swallowed uncertainly—"Ian MacPherson of Talbert Hall is a much older man."

"Is that so?" Ian fairly spat the words out. "Did he send you a picture?"

"Hardly."

He leaned across the seat, his black beard within inches of her delicate porcelain skin. "It's you who are the charlatan, Miss! If you do have letters from Ian MacPherson, they are either counterfeit or stolen. Either way, I shall have you prosecuted."

"Don't threaten me," she quavered.

"In two shakes of this lamb's tail, I'll haul you out of here and put you in chains if it suits me." He stuck out his hand. "Give me those letters."

Shaken but still defiant, Jamie reached into her purse and brought out the first of her correspondence from Ian MacPherson.

He snatched it from her, and then looked up with a wide, triumphant grin. "Just as I thought. You've picked the man's pocket."

"What man?"

"Jamie MacPherson!" he boomed. The name rolled off his tongue as if it were a delicious morsel he enjoyed more each time he tasted it. He chuckled with devilish glee. "I'll turn Jamie loose on you, that's what I'll do—and sit back and watch the fur fly." He glared at her belligerently. "What do you have to say to that?"

Jamie clutched her purse to her stomach, which was alive now with butterflies. *"I'm* Jamie MacPherson."

"You?" Ian relished her remark as if it were a hilarious joke. "A girl with a pipsqueak automobile claiming to be a member of *my* clan—and a male member at that? Get out," he commanded, his laughter turning into a growl. "I'll march you over to the jail now."

Jamie clung to the seat. "I *am* Jamie MacPherson.

I have identification! I have a landlord in London who can vouch for me." Then an idea for her salvation flashed through her mind. "I wrote letters to *you!* Two of them. 'Dear Mr. MacPherson,'" she began in a babbling quote, "'on the twenty-fourth of next month I plan to take up residence in the croft of the deceased Angus—'" She broke off, afraid suddenly that Ian MacPherson might be on the verge of a stroke.

His ruddy, rugged face had darkened by three shades of crimson. "You bloody wizard!" he roared.

Genuinely alarmed, Jamie whispered, "Why shouldn't I be me?"

"Because"—he spluttered—"you're a woman!"

"Are there no MacPherson women?" Most of her fright drained away in the face of his arrogant chauvinism. "Then either you're descended from a water horse or a devil dog."

Her easy familiarity with the names of his region's folk demons incensed him further. "What are you doing here? What do you want?"

"I told you in my letter. I've come here to take up the kind of life I've always longed for."

"Those are *Jamie MacPherson's* words." The r's rolled off his tongue like rumbling thunder. "A lone woman can't tend a croft."

"Why not?"

Her brazenness put him off, but only for an instant. "I won't allow it."

"The croft belongs to me—by your own admission."

"I'll buy up the rent."

But Jamie, who had done her homework after his first letter, replied staunchly, "The Crofters' Commission would never allow that. Neither would the Department of Agriculture, or the Land Bank, either."

A Scottish oath flew off his tongue. Then, ramming the Jeep into gear, he swung it around in the middle of the narrow street and started back the way they had come.

Jamie held onto the seat with one hand and the lamb with the other, feeling as if she had just been spewed forth from an active volcano. "I can't understand why you're so upset."

"Don't try to understand it," he barked back. "Accept it. Accept, too, that in the morning you will be on your way back to London, and there will be no arguments."

"You can't force me to leave."

"I can—and I will."

Jamie kept her chin up, but inside she was racked with doubts. Perhaps he did have the power to refute her claim on the croft. He was the head of the clan, and if he could rally enough support from the other members—of whom most, no doubt, were in one way or another dependent upon him—then he might oust her without ceremony. The very thought sickened her, and she laid her cheek against the soft fleece of the lamb and fought back her tears.

After half an hour over winding perilous roads, Ian MacPherson brought the Jeep to a stop in front of a bleak baronial mansion that towered on the brow of a hill, and appeared as if its foundations had, centuries before, taken root in the harsh land that surrounded it. Not a bush or a tree softened its austere lines. Most of the windows were narrow slits set several feet deep into the walls, and on its turretted pinnacles, flagpoles—minus their banners —pointed upward like accusing fingers at the pewter sky.

"This is Talbert Hall?" Jamie said in a faint voice.

Ian folded his hands across his broad chest. "It is. You will spend the night here. In the morning you can have your car repaired and be on your way."

Jamie bristled. "I intend to sleep tonight in my croft cottage." He might have the power to evict her in the morning, but for this one night at least she was determined to be mistress of her own domain.

"You will do as I say," Ian informed her briskly, and snatching the lamb from her, he got out of the Jeep. The dogs bounded after him, and without a glance backward at Jamie, he sauntered toward the heavy front door. Jamie shook off the jacket he had lent her and leaped out after him. In a moment she had placed herself squarely in front of him, blocking his entry into the mansion.

"You will please take me to my cottage."

Once again he impressed her with his massive presence. Looming over her, he stared her down.

"The cottage you speak of as your own," he said grimly, "is one mile and three-quarters from this spot, and Talbert Hall is its nearest neighbor. There is no heat. No running water. No electricity. For three months the place has been unoccupied . . ." —his gaze flicked over her—". . . by humans, at least. Do you think such a setting is fit for a lone woman?"

Jamie's determination faltered. It was nearly seven, and the sky was still lit with a strange gray gloom, but when night did come, she had a swift, intuitive understanding of how impenetrable and frightening it could be.

She brought up her chin. "In the morning, then."

"In the morning," he said with steel in his voice, "you will be leaving."

The room to which Jamie was shown for the night was surprisingly cheerful. A bright fire danced on the tiled hearth, and thick, furlike rugs covered the icy stone floors. Indeed, the whole interior of Talbert Hall—or at least the part Jamie had been allowed to glimpse as she was hurried up the stairs by the housemaid Ian had put in charge of her—had amazed her.

In contrast to its gloomy exterior, the foyer, the great entry hall, and the several rooms opening off it that she had viewed briefly had been decorated with a hand that knew color. In impressive sections the walls were paneled with glowing golden wood. The handsome old chairs that stood like stalwart sentinels along the walls were upholstered in vibrant tapestries, and vases of fresh-cut flowers stood on every table, perfuming the air.

Standing now in her bedroom, Jamie looked dizzily about her. Was she really inside that bleak-looking stone shell that had so dismayed her a few minutes before? Her gaze went longingly to the high, four-postered bed covered over with a deep wine-colored comforter. She was weary to the bone. She felt, in fact, as if she had been shot out of a cannon to the moon, and the prospect of being catapulted back to earth again in the morning exhausted her even more. And where were her things if she must spend the night here?

In answer to her question, there was a gentle tap on the door, and the little maid, who called herself Angela, appeared again.

"Madam," she said, coming into the room on softly slippered feet, "I have brought up this one case, which I judged to hold your night things—"

"Yes, thank you." Jamie reached for it gratefully. "You needn't trouble yourself about anything else. This is all I need."

The girl snapped berry-black eyes. "Dinner, madam. In half an hour I shall bring it up."

"Oh—" Jamie hesitated. She had been bracing herself for the ordeal of dining with Ian. Now it seemed she would be eating alone, and she wondered at her disappointment. "I'm to have dinner up here, then?"

The girl seemed embarrassed. "Yes, madam. Downstairs, you see, everything is ready for the reception honoring Mr. MacPherson." Her berry eyes widened, and her hand went to cover her lips. "I'm sorry, madam—"

"About what?" Jamie's interest quickened. Was there to be a party for one of her kinsmen? "Which Mr. MacPherson is being honored?"

"You, madam," the girl said in a small voice. "You that was supposed to be him, I mean." The girl backed off. "I'll be going to see about your supper."

"Angela—" Jamie smiled encouragingly. "Are you saying that Mr. MacPherson—Mr. *Ian* MacPherson—has arranged a reception for Jamie MacPherson?" The girl's distressed look gave her her answer.

"But now that Jamie MacPherson has turned out to be a woman, the reception is off?"

"Oh, no madam! The guests are coming in like sheep to the fold this very minute." Angela's face lit up. "Oh, you should see them, all grand in their kilts, and some with bagpipes, even. Lor, the ghosts will fair sit up tonight."

Ghosts. Jamie laughed. "But if the party is going on as planned, am I not to be invited?" Surely Ian was not so much a child that he couldn't gracefully admit to his guests that he had made a mistake and at least let her enjoy her own party before he sent her packing. "Tell your master I'll be down soon."

The girl paled. "Oh, no madam! It isn't that kind of reception. There are only men. They'll eat and drink and best each other with stories—"

Jokes, she means. Jamie understood at last. In honor of his arriving clansman, Ian had arranged a bachelor party. No wonder he was put out with her!

She let the girl go then, and as soon as the door was closed she went quickly to the narrow windows and peered out. But darkness had fallen and evidently her bedroom faced a direction other than the entry, for there was no sign of life in the black glare that looked back at her from the other side of the glass. She felt as isolated as if she were locked in a dungeon.

Her dinner arrived shortly, however, and intrigued by the assortment of strange foods she had read about but had never tasted, she forgot her misery for a time and filled her stomach.

Bolstered by the meal, her first since morning, she let herself down in the hot tub Angela had drawn for her in the surprisingly luxurious bathroom and soaked for a time, admiring the delicate blue and white tiles that lined the tub alcove and were reflected in the mirrors that covered the other walls. A crystal bottle of toilet water graced the dressing table, and after Jamie had toweled dry with a woolly soft bath sheet, she splashed the fragrance all over her body, reveling in its mimosa sweetness. Whoever had supplied it had a taste that matched her own, Jamie decided, and wondered if she would ever be wealthy enough to buy so compelling a scent for herself.

Coming out of the bathroom, she caught the faint sounds of laughter and the discordant tones of the bagpipes below. Her heartbeat quickened. The party. It must be in full swing by now. Hastily, she dressed in the warmest of her nightgowns, wrapped a robe around her shoulders, and stole out into the hallway.

Positioning herself in the shadows toward the left of where the stone steps rose from the entry hall, Jamie peered down into the sea of light below her and partway into a room which had not been open on her arrival. A dizzying array of plaid kilts moved like patterned fish across her sphere of vision, and through the constant roar of talk and laughter she heard the joyous blasts of the bagpipes.

What a glorious time they were having! Wistfully, Jamie leaned forward, eager to snatch every glimpse she could of the merriment below. If only for this one night she could have been a man! Amongst all those hardy MacPhersons she could have found the answers to the questions that had puzzled her all her life about her family history. She was kin to those dozens of men milling about down there—by less than a single drop of blood in most cases, but kin, nevertheless. They shared with her the same ancestry, the same name. They were Ian's "flock," and whether he liked it or not, she was a part of that flock, too—if no more than the lost lamb! A sudden surge of anger blocked her breathing. How dare that arrogant, domineering male relegate her to the upstairs as if she were a child, when the party given in her honor was reaching its glorious climax below!

Then, suddenly, one man stood out alone in the center of the hall. Ian—in the kilted splendor of ceremonial dress that included a lace-edged shirt and a silver-buttoned jacket that closed over his wide chest. His thick, black hair turned up at the edge of his collar and framed his strong jaw, giving him an aura of power that set Jamie's heart pounding. Then all at once his gaze lifted and fixed itself on the shadow in which she crouched.

Jamie shrank back. Despite the distance that separated them, the depth of that gaze had a searching quality. She felt it pulling her, and it was all she could do not to rise and make herself known.

When Ian turned away at last, Jamie wilted in the darkness as though the sustaining strength in her body had been withdrawn. For long minutes afterward she knelt, trembling, unable to fathom the curious yearning that possessed her.

Chapter Two

Dawn crept into Jamie's room in Talbert Hall long before she awoke, and when finally she sat up, blinking in the soft light, she was aware, though it was only seven, that the sun had been up for hours.

Dressing herself in the same close-fitting black trousers and checked weskit and jacket she had worn the day before, she brought a ribbon around in a bow beneath the collar of her shirt, and with another pulled back her shining black hair into a ponytail. Surveying herself in the mirror over the dressing table, she decided she looked none the worse for the prior day's misadventures and let herself out into the hall.

Not an echo was left of the night's riotous clamour, and for a moment Jamie hesitated at the head of the stairs, feeling as if a spell had been cast over the castle and that only she—tucked in with the hot-water bottle between the flannel sheets Angela had turned back—had escaped the hundred-years' sleep that still held the place in thrall.

But almost at once she became aware of whispery movements below and saw that a cluster of house-maids were busily setting things in order. One was at work polishing the metal hardware of the hearth, another winding the grandfather clock, and two more dusting and sweeping.

Jamie's appearance among them produced a flurry of dipping heads and apologies and a startled exchange of looks.

"Breakfast is served at nine, madam," one ventured.

Nine! In London Jamie would have already been checking her cash drawer and straightening her stock on the shop's narrow shelves. "I've just come down to look around a bit," she said as confidently as she could and sailed past them as if she had every right to be nosing about an hour and a half before anyone else was even up. Perhaps as long as Ian MacPherson did not appear, she did have that right. At any rate, she intended to see all that she could of his lair before he loosed his wrath once more upon her.

Taking the rooms one by one, she made her way across the first floor of Talbert Hall. There was a smoking room, a billiard room, a butler's pantry, a gun room, a library, a large drawing room, and beside that the smaller one into which she had gazed last night, a dining room, and a lesser room beyond which she refrained from entering because two more maids were busily setting the table there.

Everywhere there were enormous fireplaces, some of which were banked with greenery in anticipation of the spring that had not yet arrived, and others blazed with comforting fires in acknowledgment of yesterday's wintry blast.

The sun, however, was shining today, and noting the inviting fingers of light that beckoned in the large drawing room, Jamie crossed to the windows to look out.

What she saw was as astonishing as the bleak face the castle had presented the evening before. The back side of Talbert Hall—a rolling sweep that dropped off into shadowy glens—was a veritable paradise. A high stone wall surrounded it, and within the wall's boundaries budding rhododendrons as tall as houses blocked out the dreary gray of the stones. Eucalyptus, bamboo and azaleas spaced formal beds of annuals just coming into flower, and a single white rose bush, larger than the abandoned Austin, bore on its upper branches half a dozen blossoms the size of dinner plates. Beyond this, Jamie saw the glint of sun on a greenhouse and inside its glass walls a rainbow of colors that accounted for the fragrant bouquets enhancing the rooms of the hall.

Enchanted, she let out a low moan of delight that was immediately echoed by a deeper sound—though not one of pleasure.

"So you're here," a clipped voice said behind her.

Whirling, Jamie saw that a man had entered the room and had it not been for the piercing blue gaze he fixed upon her, she would have been uncertain that it was Ian.

"You've shaved your beard!" she exclaimed.

"And trimmed my hair, as well," he answered briskly. "The occasion for the growth of both is past."

"The party last night?" she said, unable not to admire his clean-shaven good looks. She could scarcely believe this urbane, polished laird of the manor dressed in close-fitting riding pants and suede jacket was the same woolly bear who had rescued her yesterday.

He disdained an answer to her question and went around her to pull back one of the heavy tapestry draperies that had remained closed. "Sun," he said with satisfaction. "Your journey back to London should be pleasant."

Jamie swallowed. "Ian—Mr. MacPherson—you're being unreasonably stubborn. I've a right to be here, you know. I came at your invitation."

He scowled. "I did not invite you. I invited a fellow clansman whom I hoped would take up the croft and settle here."

"I hope to settle here," she said, amazed at her own daring. "Certainly I intend to stay the year out."

"Not on my land."

"It isn't your land! You told me yourself that Jamie MacPherson had inherited the tenure of the croft and could remain on it as long as the rent was kept up." Her voice grew stronger. "I know the rent is only a few pounds. There's every possibility I may stay on for years."

"Over my dead body!"

Jamie felt herself gaining ground. "I shan't require that great a sacrifice. But a little courtesy might be in order. After all, I am a MacPherson—though only a lowly female—and I suspect that if our clansmen knew I was here, I would have received a far warmer welcome than you have extended."

Ian's ruddy face took on a scarlet hue. "What makes you think they don't know?"

On Jamie's part the remark had been a shot in the dark, but seeing Ian's reaction, she was delighted to have fired it. "It was far easier, wasn't it, to say that your guest of honor had at the last minute canceled plans to come to Scotland than to explain that you'd tucked your mistake away upstairs?"

"I did not make a mistake." Ian eyed her icily. "You misled me."

"Oh, no—I won't let you get away with that! I never in any way indicated that I was a man. You thought of that yourself."

Ian glared at her, but Jamie felt sure enough of herself to relax a little and return the gaze with a look of forthright inspection. There was no denying that Ian MacPherson was an impressive-looking man. Without the tangled beard and long curling locks that had startled her yesterday, Ian's countenance had assumed an even more compelling attractiveness. The bright blue eyes were the same, and so was the sensuous mouth, but a stubborn cleft chin and a strong jaw had emerged. His neck was thick and powerful, and he moved with a virile assurance that excited her. Jamie flushed as a devilish trick of mind caused her to imagine suddenly the pleasure that a kiss from such a man might bring.

Sensing that in some way he had regained lost territory, Ian resumed the argument. "I explained last night that for you to stay in the cottage is out of the question."

"That's for me to decide, isn't it?" Jamie had put off thinking of the inconveniences he had described, but in the sunny light of morning they seemed less depressing, and she took heart. "If other women can manage, I'm sure I can, too."

"Other women have men to tend the chores."

"If necessary, I'll hire someone to have my chores done."

He gave her a swift look. "You might find that rather expensive."

Jamie flushed. He had seen her scuffed suitcases and the battered Austin and concluded rightly that her purse was pinched.

Then a sudden inspiration seized her. "I shan't be using my grazing rights or planting a crop on my four acres. It's not unrealistic, is it, to assume that another crofter might welcome those privileges in exchange for cutting the peat for my fire and drawing a little water?"

Ian's jawline hardened. She had him, she saw with a surge of triumph, and it was all she could do not to laugh. But then just as swiftly she felt a wave of compassion for the proud, angry man who stood before her. Though it was not her fault, she had caused him discomfort last night, and now if she stayed on there would be no way for him to avoid some sort of explanation to those who believed Jamie MacPherson had never arrived. She should not forget, either, that if he had not come along and offered her a ride into Applecross, she might have spent the night by the side of the road rather than in the warm, comfortable bed where she had lain, instead.

"Look here," she said, offering her hand in a spontaneous gesture of friendship. "Can't we declare a truce? After all, we're kinsmen."

"That's a matter for conjecture," he said gruffly, but nevertheless he took her hand, and when it was enclosed in his warm, strong clasp, he seemed, for a moment, reluctant to let it go.

Jamie, too, was caught up in the touch of his flesh upon hers, and her usually reliable heart began to flutter. Swiftly, she changed the subject. "Your garden—" She turned toward the window, taking her hand with her to gesture toward the blooming rose bush. "It's lovely—and quite unexpected."

He said in a tone still gruff, "How do you mean?"

"It's such a contrast to the approach we made yesterday." She floundered, embarrassed all at once to admit how dreary she had thought the castle looked without a bush or a tree to soften its harsh lines. "I never expected such lushness," she finished lamely.

"That's as it should be." His tone softened somewhat, but he held on to his air of disapproval. "Talbert Hall is an ancient fortress. It is in its character to be forbidding. It would be improper for it not to present a formidable face to those who approach it. But that doesn't mean that we Scotsmen don't appreciate beauty."

His throat darkened suddenly, and Jamie, amused that he had included her in the sacred inner circle of his heritage and at the same time given her a kind of left-handed compliment, came to his rescue.

"I understand. I've made a study—limited, of course—of my ancestors, and I know how well balanced the nature of the Scotsman is. There's keenness tempered with compassion, shrewdness with wit, valor with tenderness—" Her voice trailed off, and she experienced her own moment of embarrassment.

This time it was Ian who rescued *her*. "—And starkness tempered with lushness." Unexpectedly, they both laughed, and Jamie saw that she had pleased him with her little speech.

She was delighted when he went on to say, "After

breakfast I'll show you the garden. It was, by the way, designed and planted by Angus MacPherson's grandfather. You might find an additional interest in it on that account."

On that generous note they went in to breakfast— a hearty meal composed of kippers under a silver-plated cover, mushrooms and kidneys, and jumbo grilled sausages. Jamie, who was accustomed only to tea and jam-spread toast, nevertheless ate with gusto, the spark of hope generated by the pleasant conclusion to their talk whetting her appetite.

Afterward, they went for the stroll Ian had promised through rows of daffodils just beginning to show their gold and along patches of neatly planted turnips. Ian, visibly more affable as the tour progressed, explained how it was possible to create a near-tropical paradise in the formidable climate of the Highlands.

"The Scotch pines are responsible," he commented, pointing beyond the wall to a dense, sheltering belt of vigorous growth. "The prevailing winds—and sleet, too, I might add—come from that direction. The trees act as a buffer and combine with the wall to create their own climate."

"And a fortunate climate it is," said Jamie, placing admiring fingertips on the velvet petals of a white narcissus.

Ian stooped and broke it off for her. When he put it into her hand, their eyes met, and Jamie felt the same compelling power of his gaze that had almost caused her to surrender her position at the top of the stairs the evening before.

That thought brought to mind an apology she felt

she must make. "I spied on you last night," she said, dipping pink cheeks to the flower. "It was such a joyous-sounding party I simply couldn't resist. I'm afraid I crept out and hid at the top of the stairs for a time."

Ian looked down at her, a bemused expression on his sensuous mouth. "I know. I was aware of your presence there."

Jamie, remembering his steadfast gaze as she crouched in the shadows, caught her breath. "You knew I was watching? How?"

The look on his lips became a faint smile. "The mimosa perfume. I caught its scent."

"Mercy!" A flush rose from Jamie's throat. "I must have drowned myself in it."

"Not at all. I'm sensitive to that fragrance. It's one I'm fond of."

"So am I." Jamie's cheeks brightened. "That is, I've never used it before, but I loved it the moment I lifted the stopper."

His eyes held to her face while she spoke, and then his voice took on a disturbing huskiness. "You must have a bottle for yourself, then. You wear it well."

They walked on in an uncomfortable silence, Jamie wondering at the complex man who strode along beside her. One moment he seemed as fierce as an ancient Scottish chieftain and she shrank from his abrasiveness. Then in the next moment she felt drawn to him, desperate almost to glimpse behind that handsome facade and discover why he reacted to her with such hostility.

Finally, unable to hold back her anxiety any longer, Jamie blurted out, "Please let me stay, Ian.

You can't imagine what it means to me to be here at last. I've schemed and dreamed—" Her words tumbled out. "I've used all my savings to buy the Austin, I've given up my flat and resigned myself to this situation. I can't go back to London."

Ian folded his arms and kept his level gaze on the pink buds of a cherry tree. "It is my intention that a man should occupy the cottage," he said stubbornly.

"I realize that. I know my coming has been disrupting and a disappointment. The crofts are dying, I know that; and I know how vital it is to encourage the return of those to whom they once belonged—but I'm one of those. Please recognize that. I want to be here. What difference does it make which sex I am?"

He settled a brooding look on her. "I wonder—" he said darkly. "I wonder how much difference it will make."

The words were heavy with portent, but that escaped Jamie entirely. She heard only his use of the future tense and seized upon that as a sign of yielding. In a burst of joyous abandon, she threw her arms around his waist and pressed her face to the male smoothness of his suede coat.

"Thank you, Ian! Oh, thank you! I'll take wonderful care of the place. I promise. And I won't mind at all how isolated it is. I'll need to be alone, anyway, for my painting." She lifted her face, her violet eyes starry. "We'll be wonderful friends. You'll see."

In her unbridled delight, Jamie had not noticed that Ian had matched her gesture with an embrace of his own. Now she felt his arms tighten about her waist. An electric thrill shot through her as their glances locked. She waited breathlessly for the kiss that seemed imminent.

But abruptly Ian released her. Turning away, he said in a remote tone that chilled her through, "Nothing is settled yet."

As the Jeep with Ian behind the wheel wound over the gnarled hillsides of the Talbert Hall estate, Jamie found it almost unbelievable that yesterday a bitter wind carrying sleet had whipped across the countryside. Now the sun was shining brightly, and if its rays were not exactly warming, at least there was no biting chill in the air.

Between the gaunt mountains ahead the small secluded valleys, that in the Highlands were called glens, beckoned invitingly. Black-faced sheep from the Hebrides and white-faced Cheviots grazed with placid assurance on neighboring hillsides. Everywhere a natural grandeur blended with tranquility.

"Is it much farther to my cottage?" said Jamie, and then at once she regretted her phrasing. Perhaps she was pushing things to label the cottage hers. Only an hour had passed since Ian had agreed to let her see it, and—as he had said—nothing had actually been settled. But the fact that he was driving her there was encouraging. Unable to restrain herself, she added, "I can't wait until we get there."

"Only a minute more." Ian's tone was pleasant enough, but the set of his jaw worried her. Another nagging doubt dimmed her excitement, too. Several of the croft houses they had passed on this long way around before they came to her Uncle Angus's were deserted and badly in need of repair. If her own appeared in a similar condition, how would she keep up a positive front before Ian? He had warned that the cottage was primitive. Had he meant there were holes in the roof? Or mice, even?

Jamie shuddered, but she was determined, no matter what the condition of the cottage, to claim it, and she held on to her smile, adding a jaunty little tune beneath her breath to reassure herself.

Then all at once they came up over a rise and Ian halted the Jeep before a freshly white-washed stone cottage tucked snugly against the side of a hill.

"Here we are," said Ian and got out. Wide-eyed, Jamie scrambled out behind him.

"Do you mean this is it? This adorable place is what you've been making such dour pronouncements about?"

The cottage was in excellent condition—from its thatched roof protected from the wind by a stone-weighted net, to the neat little flowerbed bordering its sides.

Jamie breathed in delight. "It's beautiful!"

"You wouldn't have said so a month ago," Ian remarked curtly. Taking a key from his pocket, he unlocked the door. "Angus wasn't much of a house-keeper. The smoke on the walls was an inch thick."

There was no smoke now, Jamie saw. Every wall had been scrubbed and painted to match the white exterior. In the main room a sofa, two chairs and a lamp table were arranged cozily before a peat fire crackling in the hearth. The kitchen area was shiny and spotless, and beyond, in the bedroom, Jamie glimpsed a coverlet the color of sunshine spread over a bed. There was a rocker with a matching footstool, and in another corner was a washstand with bowl and pitcher. In both rooms braided rugs dotted the newly swept floor.

"What a lot of trouble you've gone to!" Not for her, of course, Jamie admitted wistfully. But what did that matter if she were the one to enjoy it?

Ian spoke gruffly. "Your uncle's things are packed away in a box in the cupboard. He left little behind. He lived a sparse life."

Moved suddenly by the thoughtfulness that had gone into making the cottage comfortable and welcoming, Jamie laid her hand on his arm. "I know your preparations weren't for me, but I thank you just the same." She waited a moment. "I can stay, can't I?"

He looked down at her and with a sardonic twist to his lips said, "You're a MacPherson. There'll be no budging you now that you've seen it, I'd imagine."

Jamie was torn between laughing and crying. For Ian the words were tantamount to surrender, and she knew he had paid a dear price to say them. "You won't be sorry," she assured him, and with glowing eyes returned his look. Then aware all at once of her hand on his arm, she withdrew it hastily and put it behind her. "When may I move in? Today?"

His curt reply startled her. "There'll be a week's delay, at least. There's more work to be done."

Jamie's eyes widened. "I can't imagine what. Everything is spotless and in perfect order, as far as I can see."

"You don't see a bathtub, do you?" he said harshly.

Jamie was amused. "I can do without that. The weather will soon be warm. I can bathe in the river." She smiled impishly. "In the meantime, there's always the pitcher and bowl."

"You will not move your things here until the plumbing is completed," he answered with uncompromising firmness. "Roughing it for a man is one thing, but a woman requires something less primitive."

"Ian—you've done enough. I'm grateful. Now, if you will simply forget that I'm a woman—"

He turned his blue eyes upon her, and she saw with a shock that they were smoldering. "How can I do that?" he said. "I smell your scent, I look at your skin as delicate as fine china, I hear your voice—"

Jamie stared at him dumbly.

"Do you imagine that I'm blind—or totally insensitive?" His nostrils flared. "You are very much a woman—and I am very much aware of it."

Jamie moistened her lips. "If my presence disturbs you—"

"What will you do?" he demanded coldly. "Go back to England? I requested that. You refused."

Jamie's thoughts whirled. "Surely we can be friends—" But the moment the words were out, her quickening senses refuted them. With another shock she realized she wanted much more than friendship from Ian MacPherson. She wanted to respond physically to the compelling power of his gaze. She wanted to know his embrace, his lips on hers . . .

They faced each other, the charged distance between them drawing them together like a magnet. Suddenly they were in each other's arms.

With a jolt Jamie realized she had always known Ian's kiss. She had dreamed of it, she had felt its shape, she had tasted it in a thousand moments of secret yearning before she had ever laid eyes on him.

His mouth moved on hers, and she knew the next movement before it began. She felt the thrill of his flesh on hers before his hand slid to the nape of her neck. His arms were created to hold her. . . . She belonged next to the heavy pounding of his heart. . . .

Ian pulled away, his blue eyes veiled. In a voice as impersonal as if he had only shaken her hand or opened a door for her, he said, "There. Now you've been initiated into the clan."

Jamie recoiled. *That was all his kiss had meant?* She steadied herself with a hand on the table. "You needn't have troubled yourself."

"No trouble." His idle gaze slid over her. "I found kissing you quite pleasant, in fact."

Pleasant! Jamie took a deep breath and stared straight into his mocking eyes. "Shall I make a pot of tea?"

Her aplomb took him back, but he covered his surprise quickly. "How do you know the caddy's not empty?"

"I can't imagine that it would be." She eyed him coldly. "You've thought of everything, haven't you?" Turning away, she moved toward the kitchen. The devil was in him, kissing her with such passion! But now she understood. That was his vengeance. He was making her pay for being a woman. Well— he'd never have the chance again. She'd make certain of that.

With trembling fingers she brought the mugs from the cupboard and filled a kettle from the reserve of water she found in a stone crock on the drainboard. The low fire some hand other than hers had lit earlier came to life under her coaxing, and in a few minutes Jamie served tea to Ian by the hearth, where he had gone to sit while she stirred around in the kitchen. When he took the cup from her, their eyes met briefly, but Jamie had brought herself under control, and she returned his gaze coolly.

"Do you take sugar?"

He shook his head, and she sat down. "What shall I do about my car?"

Keeping his eyes on the steam rising from his cup, he said evenly, "It's repaired by now, I imagine—and waiting for you at the Hall."

"Really?" Gratitude swept over Jamie, despite her anger. "You saw about it this morning?"

"Last night. One of our men is quite a good mechanic. I mentioned it to him as he was leaving the party and he promised to take care of it." Ian shot her a coldly challenging look. "You see, you are mistaken. I made no effort to hide your presence from my guests."

Jamie flushed. "Did you tell them I lied to you?"

"Should I have?"

"You know the answer to that!"

"I told them you were exhausted and had gone to bed." He eyed her with a faint smile of satisfaction. "When they learned you were a woman, they understood, of course."

Jamie bristled. "I think you ought to at least have introduced me. You needn't have worried I'd linger and mar the revelry."

He came back at her easily. "How could I be sure? You managed nicely to mar most of my afternoon."

Jamie wanted to throw something at him, but

instead she stood up and said, "I think we should go. If you intend to set a plumber working here, you should start him without further delay."

Ian set down his mug. "Are you giving me orders?"

"I'm suggesting—"

His voice became stony. "I can do without suggestions, too, thank you."

Jamie saw she had made him furious and was delighted. She said tauntingly, "Sometimes suggestions can be quite helpful."

"If I judge they will be, I shall ask for them."

Jamie smiled. "Just let me know."

"Look here—" Ian's face had turned scarlet. "I have allowed you to have your way in the matter of the cottage. I have arranged for your car to be repaired, and I will see to it that there is running water in this place before the weekend, but I will not be ordered about or baited by a girl! Do you understand that?"

"With your shouting in that way," she retorted calmly, "how can I help it?"

"You haven't heard anything yet!" he thundered. "But if you persist in annoying me, I shall crack your eardrums."

Jamie marched past him to the door. "Go right ahead. I shan't mind being deaf for evermore, as long as it's *your* voice I won't have to listen to."

They rode back to the castle in a heavy silence. Jamie was aware of the ribbons of frothing water dancing along in a burn beside the Jeep and of church spires in the distance. She knew that the scenery unfolding around her was lovely in the way

of the harsh grandeur that typefied the Highlands,
but she kept her eyes on the road, her mouth in a
tight straight line.

Ian MacPherson was the most insulting man she
had ever met. He was an arrogant, childish beast.
The less she saw of him, the happier she would be.
When she was free of him at last and on her own, her
door would never be open to him, no matter that he
was her landlord and head of the clan and laird of
the estate. He was a despicable, conceited chauvin-
ist, and she would have no more to do with him than
was absolutely required.

She had worked up as much steam as the kettle by
the time they arrived back at Talbert Hall, but when
Jamie saw a shining Rolls-Royce parked before the
entrance, she smoothed back her hair and put on a
less strained expression.

"You have guests," she commented without looking at Ian.

"Avril," he replied tonelessly.

Unconsciously, Jamie tensed. *Who was Avril? A
woman he kissed and meant it?*

As if he had heard her question, Ian said, "She
lives in the village. She's Lady Stuart, actually."

"I see." Jamie relaxed, picturing a graying dowager with a poodle under her arm. "Shall I go straight
upstairs? Or will you have me meet her?"

Ian said dryly, "I assumed, of course, that you'd
do just as you pleased."

"That's most unfair!"

"But accurate, nevertheless. However, let's declare a truce, shall we?" He barely suppressed a
sigh. "At least until Avril is gone."

Jamie nodded stiffly, but secretly she was pleased.

His comment had been unfair, but at least he had recognized her spirit and even shown a hint of respect for it. She allowed him a thin smile. "You may tell Lady Stuart whatever you like about my arrival."

Ian shot her a dark look. "Thank you very much."

Jamie's smile widened. "Not at all."

Chapter Three

"Well, Avril—you're up early this morning."

With Jamie trailing him, Ian advanced across the small drawing room toward a female figure seated on a sofa with a picture album in her lap. "What are you doing? Reminiscing?"

The person he had addressed as Avril looked up. "I'm killing time, actually, waiting for you. I'm dying to know how things went last night—" Her smile of greeting faded as she became aware of Jamie. "Sorry—" The warmth left her voice. "I didn't realize you had a guest."

"Jamie MacPherson," Ian announced dryly. "So you can imagine how things went last night."

Avril's gaze swept over Jamie. "A *woman?*"

Ian laughed. "How astute you are, my dear. Precisely—a woman." He turned to Jamie. "May I present Lady Avril Stuart? She made most of the arrangements for last night's festivities; hence, her . . ."—he cleared his throat—". . . her rather blunt greeting."

Jamie felt heat scalding her cheeks. Instead of the graying matron she had pictured as Avril Stuart, the slim blonde beauty scrutinizing her was only a few years older than herself and, she felt, infinitely more attractive. Avril wore an expensive dress of tissue wool in shades of heather and rose. Her hair was swept high on her head in an elegant twist, and it was clear that she regarded Jamie as an intruder.

Nevertheless, she offered an apology. "I'm afraid you took me by surprise, Miss MacPherson. I was expecting someone burly and brutish like Ian."

Ian pretended offense. "Burly and brutish!"

With a conspiratorial air plainly meant to exclude Jamie, Avril slid her eyes over Ian's lean, athletic body. She stood up and slipped her arm into his. "Appear with a woman at your side when I am expecting a man, darling, and I will label you brutish every time."

Wincing at the heavy-lidded look with which Ian responded to Avril's remark, Jamie said, a bit too loudly, "I'm sure you have things to discuss. Please excuse me."

"No, no—" Avril's sculpted lips turned up in a smile that was unaccountably affable. "Stay, won't you? I'm eager to hear how it happens you're at Talbert Hall and Jamie MacPherson is not."

"I *am* Jamie MacPherson, Lady Stuart."

"Yes, of course." Avril's silky voice came at her soothingly. "But I wonder why it never occurred to either Ian or me that you might be female."

"I can't imagine," said Jamie stiffly, resenting Avril's intimation that she had a part in everything that concerned Ian. "Mine is not an unusual name for a woman."

"It was your father's name, was it not?" said Ian.

Jamie flushed. "What difference does that make?"

"I assume he wanted a son."

Jamie kept her gaze level. "If he did, he never said so."

Avril intervened with her silken tone. "So you simply arrived here on the doorstep. What did *you* do, darling?" she said to Ian.

"Actually, I picked her up on the road," he answered.

"How fascinating!"

Jamie glared. "My car broke down."

Without inviting Jamie to be seated, Ian threw himself onto the couch, and Avril took the place beside him. "I brought her here—after we detoured by way of Applecross—and the party went on as scheduled." Ian gave Jamie a careless glance. "She didn't attend, of course."

Avril covered a trill of laughter with a slender hand pressed to her lips. "I should think not!" She turned to Jamie. "I'm sure it was quite a ribald affair. Nothing you would have enjoyed."

"I would have enjoyed meeting my kinsmen."

"There'll be ample time for that," Ian said gruffly.

"You're staying?" Avril sat forward, suddenly tense. "Surely not at the croft."

"Why not?" said Jamie. "It's quite cozy and comfortable."

"I'm putting in water," said Ian curtly. "She's determined to have a go at it. We'll let her see how she likes it."

Jamie, thoroughly fed up with Ian's referring to her as if she were absent or had no brains at all, said hotly, "I can tell you how I'll like it—wonderfully well! Now, if you will tell *me*, Mr. MacPherson, where I might find my car, I'll get my things and go there now."

Ian scowled and got to his feet. "You're not going until the end of the week. We've settled all that."

"You've settled it. I have other plans."

"I shall make the plans."

"Not for me!"

Avril stood up. "My, my. You two should hear yourselves." Her eyes darted between them. "Ian, if Jamie wants to stay at the cottage, let her. I'm sure she knows far better than anyone else what it takes to make her comfortable."

"That's not the point."

"No," said Jamie. "The point is that you are to make all the decisions, and I am to meekly observe them!"

Ian glared. "I shall send someone to see about your car."

Jamie glared back. "Thank you!"

When he was gone, Jamie found she was trembling, and when Avril suggested that she sit for a minute and chat, she gratefully took the seat Ian had vacated.

Avril eyed her coolly. "What a jolly mixup this is."

"It needn't be," said Jamie, on the verge of tears. "It's Ian who's making an issue of everything."

"You don't understand him," Avril said archly. "Ian can't bear contradiction. He's proud, you see. All our men are proud."

"In my vocabulary, stubborn and proud are not synonymous."

"Perhaps that is the problem. We speak a different

language here. Women aren't nearly so forward in the Highlands as—" she paused. "You're from London, I believe?"

Jamie felt a renewal of her rage. "Does it matter where I'm from?" In her mind she contrasted the intimate way Ian had held her in the cottage to his callous treatment of her in front of Avril. "My rights as a human being should be the same here as anywhere else in the world."

"Oh, but of course they are." Avril smiled indulgently. "One simply learns a more subtle way of achieving them when one is dealing with men who are accustomed to ruling."

"Ruling! I think that's disgusting. I think it's archaic!"

Avril remained cool. "I don't dispute that. Nevertheless, it's important, I think, to recognize any situation as it actually exists, rather than as one might wish it existed." With a self-satisfied air, she turned a large diamond on her finger, and Jamie realized with a pleasant little shock that she was married.

"This is what I keep stressing to Katrine," Avril said with a sideways glance at Jamie. "But I'm afraid she's just as headstrong and independent as you."

Jamie blinked, still thinking of the ring. "Katrine?"

"My younger sister. Here—let me show you." Avril took up the picture album she had set aside when Ian and Jamie entered the drawing room and flipped through it until she came to a picture of a girl who might have been herself at eighteen or nineteen. Ian was at the girl's side. "This is Katrine. Lovely, isn't she?"

"Yes," Jamie murmured. "She's beautiful." But she was far more interested in the brooding look on Ian's face as he gazed at Avril's sister than she was in the blonde beauty who smiled up at him. She felt her throat tighten. "When was this taken?"

"Last summer. Katrine is in school in Edinburgh, but she was at home for the holidays." Avril closed the book with a sigh. "Alex and I—Alex is my husband," she said to Jamie. "We had hoped that Ian and Katrine would announce their engagement then."

"Oh—" Jamie suddenly felt as if she were suffocating. "They're to be married?"

"Oh, yes." Avril looked like a cat contemplating a dish of cream. "It's been a settled fact for ages, but for one reason or another they keep putting off setting a date. It's Katrine's fault, of course." She sighed. "Ian is mad for her, naturally, but she's such a saucy girl and so high-spirited—much like—"

She broke off abruptly and Jamie finished for her in a lifeless voice. "Like me?"

Silvery laughter filled the drawing room. "I should add 'outspoken,' too! Oh, you young things. You think you have only to snap your fingers, and the man you love will come running."

I've never thought that. Nettled, Jamie wondered that Avril, who quite obviously knew how attractive she was, should deliberately classify herself as an older woman.

Avril went on. "You are simply too inexperienced to understand how demeaning it is to a man for a woman to be too assertive. Really, my dear, one can accomplish so much more with just a little cleverness." The iciness Jamie had seen at first in Avril's eyes returned. Her frosty gaze settled on Jamie. "Especially when one has looks."

Jamie stood up. "I must go. I want to be ready to leave when Ian comes back with my car."

"I hope you'll be happy at the croft," Avril said, rising beside her.

"I'm sure I shall be. Good-bye, Lady Stuart. It was pleasant meeting you."

"Oh, don't say good-bye. And please call me Avril." She smiled. *She smiled so easily*, Jamie thought. "We'll meet again soon. I'll have Ian bring you to Applecross and we can have dinner together. Alex will want to meet you, of course."

Of course, thought Jamie dejectedly as she climbed the stairs. *Alex, like everyone else, would want a glimpse of the astonishing Jamie MacPherson, whose chief appeal it seemed was that she was a she, instead of a he!*

Though Jamie was determined to get into her croft cottage at least by nightfall, fate intervened and prevented her again from doing so.

Shortly after Avril's shiny Rolls-Royce was seen disappearing down the winding road that led away from the castle, Jamie heard Angela's soft tap on the door, and when she opened it, she was given a message that the laird would like to see her in his study.

When Jamie presented herself in the book-lined room which she had not noticed on her morning tour, Ian was seated behind a scarred and cluttered desk, smoking a pipe.

"Sit down," he said without ceremony and motioned her toward a worn leather chair.

Jamie did as he bade, relaxing a little in the homey atmosphere of the room. The smell of tobacco mingling with that of leather and old books stirred pleasant memories of a cubbyhole her father had once called his den. She appreciated, too, the well-used look of the room's appointments. Clearly, it was a place not meant to impress visitors, and Jamie's opinion of Ian rose a notch. He was a man who knew how to make himself comfortable regardless of what others might think, and she liked that.

"Your car has suffered a major breakdown," Ian announced cheerfully as soon as she was seated. "Parts have been ordered from Inverness, but it may be a week before they arrive."

"A week!" Jamie sat forward. "I can't manage for a week alone on the moor without a car."

"Precisely," said Ian. "You will have to stay here. In the meantime the plumbing will be completed." He gave her a superior look. "Things have a way of working out as they should, wouldn't you agree?"

Instantly, Jamie backtracked. "I suppose I could manage, after all. I could go into Applecross today for supplies."

"Ah, but a car would be required for that, too," said Ian smugly. "You can hardly push your groceries home in a wheelbarrow."

"I thought," said Jamie coldly, "that someone here at the Hall might be kind enough to drive me in."

Ian made a clucking sound. "Too bad we didn't think of that earlier. Avril has just left. She would have welcomed you as a passenger."

"I would still need a wheelbarrow to get back,

wouldn't I?" said Jamie from between clenched teeth.

"No problem there. Avril and Alex are coming for dinner." Ian pushed away from the desk and stood up. "In the meantime, as long as you're stranded here, you might like to go with me to return the lost lamb to its mother."

Jamie had forgotten about the lamb amid the confusion that had engulfed her since her arrival. Now her face lit up as she remembered the cuddly bit of white fluff. But the moment she agreed to accompany Ian, she regretted it. As eager as she was for another look at the area that had been cloaked in sleet yesterday, she would find no pleasure in seeing it with Ian. If he hadn't the grace to take her into Applecross for supplies, he was nervy to offer to take her in the opposite direction!

Ian stared down at her. "Shall we go?"

Reluctantly, Jamie got out of her chair, but when they were outside, the dogs, already in the Jeep, greeted her joyously. The lamb climbed into her lap, and she forgot her displeasure.

"I think it's grown since yesterday!" she exclaimed to Ian.

"It ought to have," he answered briskly, starting the motor. "The boy who cared for it said it drank from bottles throughout the night."

"Poor starved thing. I wonder what its mother is thinking."

"That she's had one less to feed, probably." Ian glanced across the seat. In a deliberately offhanded manner, he said, "Avril was much impressed with you."

Jamie blinked, then looked away. *Why had they*

discussed her? What had Ian said? She made her voice calm by concentrating her attention on the lamb. "I can't imagine why."

"She thinks you're quite beautiful, for one thing." Ian turned his attention to the road. "For another, she admires your spirit."

Jamie frowned despite the compliment. "That's generous of Lady Stuart, but I must say I'm a bit surprised." She glanced boldly at Ian. "She gave me quite a lecture on subduing my independent impulses."

Ian chuckled. "Dear Avril. Always The Lady."

Jamie cut her eyes across at him. "She showed me a picture of her sister, too."

"Katrine." Ian bit down on the stem of his pipe.

"She's in school in Edinburgh, I believe?"

"Yes. Studying medicine."

"Oh." Jamie's heart began to pound. "Avril didn't mention that."

"She doesn't approve, that's why. She thinks it's a waste of time for a lady."

"I should imagine you'd approve, though." Jamie wondered at her daring. "It will be quite convenient, won't it?"

Ian's brow darkened. "In what way?"

"Talbert Hall is rather remote. Having a physician handy could be quite a boon."

"Katrine's home is in Applecross," Ian said and changed the subject abruptly. "Lean over the seat, will you, and see if that blasted boy put in my medicine kit. I'll need blue ointment for one of the sheep. If we haven't got it, we'll have to go back."

Jamie searched among an assortment of blankets

and baskets, wire and wool shears, until she located a rusty tin box. "Is this it?"

Ian rewarded her with a smile. "The very one. Now, see if the blue ointment is inside, and we'll be all set."

Jamie found the tube he wanted, and once the flock was located grazing tranquilly on the side of a hill, Ian doctored the injured sheep—quite skillfully, Jamie thought as she watched—and the lost lamb, skipping and cavorting, was returned to its somewhat bored-looking mother.

"I'm glad that's tended to," said Ian, lathering his hands with a sliver of black soap he took from the kit and then rinsing them in a noisy burn that was rushing into a pool below them. "Let's eat, shall we?"

Jamie stared at him. "What do you suggest? Grass?"

"I've brought a lunch along, of course." He gave her a sardonic smile. "I think of everything. Isn't that the way you put it?"

She flushed. "What you really excel at is making other people feel foolish."

He faced her squarely. "I suppose you're referring to the fact that I kissed you."

She hadn't been, and could have cut out her tongue for making him think that she had! "Not at all. What I meant was that you have bested me at every turn. The cottage, my car—" *Katrine,* she almost added.

"How have those things made you feel foolish?" he demanded.

"I'm accustomed to making my own arrangements, to caring for myself."

"And you're made uncomfortable—foolish feeling—when someone else does things for you?"

A wave of yearning washed over. *I could learn not to mind.* . . . "Let's skip it, shall we? I'd rather not talk about me anymore." She brought up her eyes, made a deeper violet by the midday haze that had settled over the hillside. "I already feel as thoroughly discussed as the front page of the morning paper."

Ian laughed at this frank reference to his conversation with Avril. "What a peculiar thing you are. Most women adore being talked about, don't they?" They had started down the hill toward the pool where he had parked the Jeep, and now he reached out for her hand to help her across a boggy spot. "Anyway, you'd better get used to it if you plan to stay. Not many interesting things occur to spark up our lives here." He gave her a devilish look that seemed to say he meant just the opposite. "So we welcome any diversion."

Jamie's blood pounded against her eardrums. He still held her hand, though they were on solid ground again, and the strong enclosure of his fingers around her own had set up an excitement that disturbed the beat of her heart. She changed the subject swiftly. "Is our lunch in the Jeep?"

He nodded. "Scout around while I fetch it and decide on the best spot for spreading it."

When he returned with two rush baskets, Jamie had settled on a sunny area beside the pool where several rocks, evidently scooped smooth by glaciers, seemed to have been laid there for the express purpose of seating picnickers.

"Is this satisfactory?"

He smiled agreeably. "It's a capital spot. I couldn't have made a better choice myself."

Jamie had the distinct feeling that this was not the first time he had shared lunch there, and a little of her pleasure at the way the morning was turning out dimmed. Had he brought Katrine here? And was the reason he was behaving so affably because Avril had told him that Jamie knew he was soon to be engaged? The pressure would be off then, and he could afford to be comfortable in her presence, even though he had kissed her.

She made a determined effort to stop thinking about the kiss, and about Katrine, too. "What have you brought for us?"

"Salmon sandwiches and mugs of brown beer." He sat down on a rock next to her. "How does that strike you?"

"Quite well," said Jamie, who suddenly realized she was ravenous. "But how can you have brought beer in a basket?"

Ian flipped up the lid of the larger one and brought out a small wooden keg. "As simple as that," he said. "They're made for picnics."

Picnics in the summertime with a beautiful blond girl home on her holidays. . . . Jamie looked at Ian, her violet eyes reflecting her pain. Ian returned the look. Then he said quietly, "Shall we begin?"

While they munched the delicious fare Ian's cook had produced—not only delectable sandwiches, but also, for dessert, a creamy sweet of toasted oatmeal, rum and fruit that Ian called *cranachan*—Jamie quizzed him about the territory. As she had hoped, he soon branched off into a discussion of the country's history, focusing on the battle of Culloden Moore, where Bonnie Prince Charles had led his clansmen in their last hopeless battle for independence from George II.

"We'll go to Culloden Moor one day," Ian finished, plainly flattered by Jamie's attention. Her raft of intelligent questions had generated a lively exchange of comments between them, and neither of them noticed how swiftly the afternoon was passing. Now he rose and put out his hand to help her up. "The Moor is quite an impressive place, as you'll see."

Jamie's eyes glowed. While they talked, Ian's charm had entirely captivated her. She had been able to forgive his cold treatment of her earlier—at the cottage and with Avril—and she was mainly aware of how well versed he was in his country's history and how proudly he clung to all the old traditions that she herself thought were important. Now she said, "You'll take me there? Really?"

"Of course." He held onto her hand and she saw that a blue shadow across his jaw was beginning to show traces of his heavy beard. Jamie caught the scent of his skin, and saw the fine lines that laughter had left at the corners of his blue eyes. All at once she felt breathless and pulled her hand away.

"This was an excellent picnic, Laird of Talbert Hall," she said crisply.

He stood where he was, looking down at her. "It turned out much better than I'd hoped."

Brought around by his sober tone, she met his gaze. "You expected us to quarrel again," she said flatly.

"Would it have surprised you if we had?"

"I'd rather not quarrel with you." She forced herself to speak evenly and to ignore her galloping heart. "I'd like us to be friends, as I told you earlier."

He was silent, chewing a blade of grass as his eyes moved across her face. Then, stooping to pick up the rush baskets, he broke the mood with a careless answer. "We can try. But it's only fair to warn you. I have a low flash point. You'll have to tread lightly on certain subjects."

His arrogant assurance that it was she who must tread lightly flew over Jamie like a swarm of bees. "In other words, to keep the peace one must never disagree with you. Is that it?"

He straightened, eyeing her from his full height. "There are some who manage to disagree more agreeably than others."

Avril, he meant. Or Katrine! Snatching up the blanket Ian had spread to hold their lunch, she began folding it with furious energy. Ian went toward the Jeep with the baskets, but when he was only halfway there he turned back to observe her. Her angry, flailing motions brought a faint smile to his lips that gradually widened as his gaze turned into a full-fledged grin. Whistling, he went on his way.

Chapter Four

The week of Jamie's captivity at the castle—as she chose to think of her enforced stay—passed far more swiftly than she had dreamed it would.

Avril and Alex came twice to dinner, and each time Avril went out of her way to be charming. However, Jamie found her transparency tiresome and annoying. Avril had made certain from the start that Jamie knew Ian belonged to Katrine, and she never missed an opportunity to make that point again whenever the men were out of earshot.

Alex, a clumsy but good-natured man in his sixties, looked upon his young wife as he might an exotic flower that had unexpectedly sprung up in his garden, and Jamie found his too-obvious show of admiration a bit galling, too. Nevertheless, she liked the fellow for his forthrightness and never minded listening to his talk when Avril engaged Ian in conversations of her own.

Jamie's mornings were generally occupied with strolling through the Talbert Hall gardens and greenhouse, sketchbook always in hand, or losing herself in one of the dozens of volumes of Scottish history that lined the walls of Ian's well-stocked library.

Several afternoons she rode horseback with Ian

over the heather-clad hills, noting with pleasure that where the plows had broken moorland soil, the first shoots of spring green were showing between the clods. The weather had tempered remarkably, and new lambs were bouncing on limber legs in every direction. Once Ian took her into Applecross to Avril's imposing mansion, where they watched white-winged geese skimming over the private loch that was visible through her drawing room windows.

Finally, late Saturday afternoon Jamie, leaning from the window of her bedroom to look out across the moor at a herd of deer grazing, saw coming up the road toward the castle her battered Austin and following close behind a sleek silver Ferrari.

Her eyes popped. Was that luxurious automobile the property of her mechanic? But then she saw that one of the estate men was driving the Austin, and that it was Ian who alighted from the Ferrari when the two vehicles came to a stop in front of the castle.

Hurriedly, Jamie touched a comb to her hair and then dashed down the stone steps for a look at her own car. Unlike the Ferrari, there was nothing special about the Austin, but it was all hers, and she was eager to see how it had fared during its week's sojourn in Applecross.

She had not dared think what its new parts, transported all the way from Inverness, might cost, but now the knot in her stomach reminded her this was an issue she must face. She prepared herself with a jaunty smile.

The smile changed to awe when Ian greeted her, and handing her the Austin's keys he said offhandedly, "I took the liberty of stocking up your larder while I was in town. I trust you'll find what you need."

Jamie followed his gaze to the back seat of her car, stacked with grocer's cartons that appeared to contain enough supplies for a month.

"Oh, my!" Amazed, she turned back to him. "You're wonderfully thoughtful." Ian's courteous treatment of her during the week had erased her initial resentment of him, but until now he had maintained a certain aloofness. Jamie, too, had assumed a cordial but cool attitude, and they had gotten along famously.

Even so, each time she looked at him the core of yearning that had taken over her heart when he kissed her reminded her of how strong his appeal for her was.

She had not forgotten either her response to Ian's kiss or the shock of recognizing how identical he was to the man she had dreamed of meeting one day and falling in love with. She did not take kindly to his arrogance or to his brash outbursts, which never failed to catch her off guard, but she was aware that when his crooked, sensuous mouth smiled at her, she was inclined to forgive him anything.

To cover her confusion over this latest demonstration of generosity, she said, "I must pay you for the supplies—and reimburse you for the repair bill, too, of course." Silently, she hoped she could manage both.

"The groceries are a house-warming gift," he answered. "As for the mechanic's fee, I'm afraid I failed to inquire. Next time I go into Applecross I'll ask, if you like."

"Yes, please. Thank you very much." Relieved at

having been spared the embarrassment of revealing how strained her finances were, she smiled up at him. She saw how rugged and appealing he looked in his light wool trousers and loosely woven sweater of the same green as the Scotch pines reaching skyward behind him. The moist wind had curled his black hair at the temples, and his rangy, athletic lines seemed to pulse with strength and animal magnetism.

Jamie's throat tightened. "I suppose everything is taken care of, then. I'll put the rest of my things in my bag, and then I'll be on my way."

Ian said casually, "If you're going this evening, I'll ride along, too, and have a look at the plumbing. One has to watch these fellows, you know, or they'll do less than they're paid for."

Jamie tried to keep the excitement out of her voice. "I'd enjoy having company. Will you come in your new Ferrari?"

Ian shrugged. "Actually, it isn't new. I picked it up in Edinburgh last summer, but I rarely drive it. The Jeep is handier, particularly in the winter."

They went toward the castle, Jamie walking silently beside him. *Had he gone down to Edinburgh to bring Katrine home in style?* Her heart ached. How foolish she was to continue thinking of Ian and Katrine as if she herself might play a part in the future they had planned together. When she was out of Ian's sight, she doubted if he ever gave her a thought, except a charitable one like the purchase of the groceries demonstrated. He was a gentleman, and once he had recovered from his initial dismay at discovering her to be a female, he had treated her as any gentleman would. What she must remember was that his interest in her was confined to that relationship. His kiss had only initiated her into the clan, as he had told her. She must accept that and get out of her mind all the other silly ideas that were apt to set her blood racing each time his gaze slid over her.

"Why so deep in thought?" he chided as they entered the front hall. "You're only moving across the moor, you know, not to the other side of the world." He halted, his blue eyes burning into hers. "Or perhaps you've changed your mind."

"Not at all!" Jamie forced a smile. "I've overstayed my time here as it is. And you've been terribly kind to put up with me."

His sensuous lips twitched in amusement. "Why, Miss MacPherson, how tame you've become—and in only a week."

Jamie flushed. "Perhaps you're right. Certainly a week ago I would have resented your calling me tame."

His gaze settled disturbingly upon the rise and fall of her breasts. "Could it be that you've come to appreciate your adversary?"

"Is that what we are? Adversaries?" Her color deepened.

He said lightly, "I'm joking, of course." But his eyes stayed on her. "You must admit, however, that we got off to rather a bad start."

Her heart pounded. Was he referring to their quarrels? Or to the moments he had held her in the croft cottage? She drew in her breath and with exaggerated brightness changed the subject. "I shall miss this place, with all its exquisitely decorated rooms."

Ian grimaced. "You aren't including my study, I hope."

Jamie laughed. "There's nothing exquisite about your study. However, I think it's my favorite room of all."

"I'm flattered. Everything there is of my choosing." His blue eyes passed carelessly over the tasteful appointments of the entry hall. "All the rest is Avril's doing."

Jamie could not conceal her surprise. "Avril decorated Talbert Hall?"

"She didn't tell you? I'm amazed. She loves bragging about it. She considers it her prize accomplishment of the new year. Naturally, I'm grateful. The place was falling down around me when she offered— No, I take that back—when she *insisted* that I do something about it. To top it off, she volunteered to take charge of the whole operation, so of course I took her up on it. Except in my study. She wasn't allowed to set foot in there."

Jamie wondered at the odd feeling that had come over her as he talked. Avril was indeed the doting older sister to have seen to it that Katrine's future home was correctly and elegantly refurbished. But had she done Katrine a favor? In Katrine's place, Jamie would have much preferred decorating her own home to suit herself. Then she was immediately ashamed. Avril had exercised perfect judgment in every detail. Katrine—younger, inexperienced, and with weightier problems to contend with than choosing draperies and wall coverings—no doubt had felt undying gratitude for her sister's efforts.

Still, Jamie's odd feeling persisted. "Did Avril oversee the renewal of Uncle Angus's cottage, too?"

Ian answered carelessly, "As a matter of fact, she's never been to the croft."

Jamie's pulse quickened. "The decorating there was all your own doing, then?"

"Except for one or two things that I hadn't the faintest idea about. The floor covering, for one. And the curtains. One of the women from a neighboring croft helped me out there."

A warmth settled over Jamie. The cottage and Ian's study displayed the same comfortable coziness —and now she knew why. Suddenly she was eager to be off. Turning to Ian, she said, her violet eyes smoky beneath their sooty lashes, "Since you're coming, anyway, why not stay and have supper with me?"

His glance locked with hers. "I'd like that." Then he added with a slow smile, "Can you cook?"

Jamie made a face. "Shouldn't you have asked that first and accepted afterward?"

The same charged atmosphere stood between them that had once before propelled them into each other's arms, but he made no move to draw her to him. "I'll take my chances," was all he said.

Crossing the moor, with Ian leading the way in the Ferrari, Jamie admired the soft apricot of the late-evening sky and marveled at how greenly furred the hillsides had become in only a week's time. There had been no recurrences of the inclement weather that had ushered her into the Highlands, and she had come to look forward each morning to the soft mists that hung over the glens and to the wispy clouds that took them up at midday.

The Highlands were all she had ever dreamed they

would be, and she was eager to get down to serious painting. In odd hours at the castle she had dabbled a bit in portraits, sketching from memory the gnarled face of a woman she had seen on the streets of Lochcarron, and once—drawing with heartfelt strokes—she had brought to her paper a commanding likeness of Ian. His rugged, virile looks had awakened in her a passionate interest in discovering just which of his powerful features contributed most to the effect he had upon her, but even after the drawing was completed, she had been unable to decide.

She loved his mouth, the tender way it curved at times, the crooked path it cut across his craggy jaw when he was angry. She loved the fullness of his lower lip and the proud, straight line of the upper one.

But his eyes were equally intriguing. When he looked at her, she felt he could see straight through to her soul. She had never known a blue so depthless and clear, not even in the Highland lochs. His broad brow excited her, and she was ever grateful that he had shaved off his beard and allowed her to know the firm set of his chin and jawline.

There was, in fact, nothing about him that she did not find compelling. Did Katrine know how fortunate she was? Wistfully, Jamie studied what she could see of Ian through the back window of the Ferrari. Or did her lovely rival in Edinburgh take him for granted and bury her head in her books?

Avril would like her to think so, Jamie mused, since she so frequently used her anxieties concerning Katrine's careless treatment of Ian as a reason for starting a conversation about them. Katrine was too interested in medicine, Avril constantly reiterated, but she never failed to remind Jamie before they were finished speaking that Katrine and Ian were, in spite of everything, informally engaged. Shutting off the Austin's motor, Jamie stared blankly at the white-washed cottage on the hill in front of her until a smart rap on the window startled her out of her reverie.

"Are you going to sit there goggling at the place?" Ian glared in at her with mock ferociousness. "Or are you coming inside?"

Jamie scrambled out of the car. "I was day-dreaming, I'm afraid."

In an uncharacteristic burst of playfulness, Ian suddenly took hold of her waist. "Building castles in the air, were you? Let me show you your real castle, my lady." Then, to her amazement, he swept her effortlessly into his arms and carried her the few steps to the cottage. Pushing open the door, he set her down across the threshold. "Behold—stone floors, rag rugs, a peat fire."

But Jamie, still trembling from his touch, saw only one thing. "Ian, you've added a whole new room!"

"Of course." He scowled to hide his pleasure in her excitement. "Where else would I have put the tub?"

Jamie dashed over to inspect the improvements. Where the wall between the kitchen and bedroom had stood, there were new walls that enclosed a small but perfectly outfitted bathroom set conveniently so that the pipes could accommodate both cooking and bathing. Above the wainscoting a skilled hand had applied white paper with tiny sprigs of yellow flowers. A stack of thick yellow and white towels and gleaming new plumbing facilities completed the renovations—except for one more thing.

Jamie lifted a crystal perfume bottle from the shelf above the washbasin and breathed deeply of its scent.

"Mimosa," she said, and turned to Ian with shining eyes. "You've worked a miracle and topped it off with the supreme luxury."

"Shall I duck my head modestly?" said Ian without the slightest intention of doing so. "Or shall I get on with unloading the car so that you can get on with preparing our supper?"

While Ian brought in his purchases, Jamie divided her time between stowing them away in her freshly painted cupboards and returning to see that the bathroom was still in place.

When she was finished with both exertions, she clasped her hands in awed admiration. "It's beautiful, Ian. Everything is simply beautiful."

"Stop saying that and feed me," he answered, pretending irritation. But his gaze raked her as he watched her make a saucy face in response. She wore a low-cut white blouse edged in lace, and a full, flowered skirt of yellow and white that, if he had not known better, he might have believed she had put on to blend with the colors of the cottage. Around her narrow waist she had tied a white apron.

"Come here," he commanded gruffly.

She put her hands on her hips. "Which do you want?" She had missed the subtle change in his tone. "Supper? Or someone at your beck and call?"

"I want," he said, looking steadily at her, "to put my arms around you."

"Ian—?" Her lips parted.

"Come here, I said."

As if in a dream, she crossed the space that separated them. As she neared he reached out for her hand and pulled her roughly against him.

"You make quite a picture in your housewifely gear," he muttered hoarsely.

"Do I?" She could barely breathe.

"You know exactly how you look. You know that all week you've enjoyed tormenting me."

"I don't know that. I know we've been friends—"

"Outwardly. Inwardly, we've been on fire for each other."

Had he longed for her, too? She felt as if her heart would burst. She longed for him now . . . for his mouth on hers . . . his arms tight around her. "You have a certain appeal," she admitted weakly.

He uttered a husky laugh and tightened his embrace. "A certain appeal," he said thickly. "What does that mean? That I appeal to your lips? To your throat? To your ears?" He kissed them all, lingeringly, with a leashed passion that excited her more than she had ever imagined a touch could.

With fevered yearning, he slid his hands down her body to her waist, where his fingers met, clasping it. His hot breath seared her cheek. "All of you appeals to me."

Then he kissed her fully, taking her mouth with his—moving on it so that each changing pressure spoke a new language. His hands left her waist and came up to cup her face. He held it like a flower, covering her eyelids with his kisses. His touch inflamed her. With sudden abandon, she brought her mouth to his, eagerly responding when the hardening of his thighs bruised hers. She slid her own arms up around his thick shoulders. Her fingers twined in his hair.

They swayed together, eyes closed, breath rasping when they tore their lips apart. Then, hungry for renewed touching, their mouths met again in an intricate, teasing game of arousal and withdrawal that left Jamie throbbing when Ian at last pulled away from her.

Breathless, she stood before him, suddenly frightened. *He would hurt her now as he had done before.* She braced herself to receive his cutting remark, but it did not come.

"Jamie." The sound of her name on his lips caressed her. He took her into his arms again, but gently this time, sheltering her against his chest with a tenderness he had not shown her before. He whispered against her cheek. "Are you the prize you seem to be?"

Caught up in the spell he cast, Jamie laid her fingers on his throat, attuning her own rhythms to the pulse beating there. *A prize . . . he had called her a prize. . . .*

Their lips met again. Then Ian set her in front of him and with a strong forefinger traced the delicate line of her chin. "Do you think I can live on love, you minx?" His low-pitched voice stroked her in spite of his taunt. "Go into the kitchen and cook me something."

Love. Every nerve in Jamie's body tingled. "What would you have, my lord?" she said lightly, torn between clinging to the last shred of her independence, and moving swiftly again into his arms.

Ian broke the mood. "Saddle of lamb will do as

well as anything." He contemplated the ceiling. "With it I'll have a light sauce—drop in a bit of basil there, please—and a dish of wild mushrooms alongside."

Jamie burst out laughing. "You'll settle for a bowl of boiling soup and some cheese and crackers if I'm to be the cook. When you want a saddle of lamb, you can give me a day's notice!"

She managed better than mere soup and crackers, however. Ian had brought along a bottle of French Chablis, which they tasted before they began their meal, and then they followed that with a delicious salmon pâté Jamie discovered among the tinned goods. For a finish, the Applecross bakery provided a bit of *cranachan*, the creamy oatmeal treat Ian had included. Altogether, it proved a thoroughly satisfying repast, though Jamie was scarcely aware of anything except that Ian was beside her and that they had shared moments too precious ever to be forgotten.

He stayed for a while beside the fire after Jamie put away the dishes, but he gave no indication that he wished to resume their intimacy, and Jamie, a bit let down but still content just to have him there, took a seat across from him in one of Angus's chairs and admired the firelight on his face.

"That first day—why did you let me believe you were a shepherd?" she asked him.

"Because I am," he answered, staring into the fire. "You saw my flock."

"But the estate is so big; you have so much to do managing it. Why don't you leave the care of the animals to the crofters?"

He gazed thoughtfully at the flames. "I'm a manager because I have to be. I'm a shepherd because I want to be. I inheritied my position as laird, but the same ancestors whose line I follow were men of the land. The tendency is still strong in me to nurture and encourage growth." He turned his gaze on her. "I am also a shepherd of the clan. It's important to me that the MacPhersons thrive."

"A family could be living in this croft instead of one woman alone. Is that what you're saying?"

He sighed. "A family could be, but where would it come from? There are abandoned crofts all over the estate." His jaw tightened. "You are welcome to this one. You're not displacing anyone."

She adopted a lighter tone. "No one except the Jamie MacPherson with whom you hoped to pass winter evenings playing cribbage and swapping tales."

Though they were meant to be teasing, her words had an unsettling effect on Ian. "One lone man," he said harshly. "There's little difference he would have made if he had come. It's just as well he never arrived."

Ian's speech deflated Jamie. She had thought he might at least flatter her with an assurance that her presence was more agreeable to him than the one he had imagined when he wrote to Jamie MacPherson, but instead she had annoyed him by reminding him of how desolate much of the Highlands had become since the younger men had begun leaving the land.

She changed the subject quickly, inquiring about aspects of croft life she felt she should know in order not to offend her neighbors. Ian explained the grazing rights, told her that her nearest neighbors were Robert and Isabel, and that they were the parents of three children, but the warmth had gone out of his voice, and shortly he rose to leave.

Jamie rose beside him. "Can't you stay a while longer?"

He shook his head. "It's late. I have tax records to go over, and men are coming in early tomorrow to discuss a disputed boundary."

"A full day," said Jamie, her heart sinking. He would have no time for her. "But perhaps you'll come again soon—when you aren't so busy."

"You'll be busy, too." His gaze rested briefly on her. "With your painting."

Watching as the Ferrari turned around in the lane and sped off over the moor, Jamie swallowed past the lump in her throat. What had gone wrong? There had been such warmth between them. But he had not touched her after supper. Nor had he kissed her good night.

With a hollow feeling, she turned from the door and closed it against the darkness. Inside her cottage, shadows from the fire danced on the ceiling and the lamplight gleamed cozily. She had dreamed for months of this moment, when all alone she could claim the croft as her own. Instead, she had never felt more miserable in her life.

Chapter Five

In the weeks that followed Jamie's evening spent with Ian, her thoughts were haunted by his abrupt departure. While she made her bed and swept her cottage, while she arranged field flowers in a blue cup on her table and kneaded bread on the kitchen drainboard, her main concern was with Ian and his puzzling behavior.

He had kissed her passionately and held her tenderly. He had whispered that she was a prize. He had even spoken of love. Then as carelessly as he might have switched off a light, he had withdrawn from her and gone his dark and brooding way back to Talbert Hall, and she hadn't seen him since.

What did he imagine she was thinking out here all alone on the moor? she wondered angrily. Or had he remembered her existence at all?

Then she was furious with herself. She had been a fool to spoil their lovely evening with talk that she knew would upset him. More than once when she was at the castle Ian had mentioned with annoyance the growing tendency of the young crofters to leave the land. There was no need for them to go to the cities, he insisted. They could make a living as others before them had by hiring themselves out part-time as fishermen or joining crews of roadmen, or even by adopting a trade in the village and returning to the crofts on the weekends. Even more, he deplored the numbers of them who were moving to other countries.

"Times had changed," Jamie had offered mildly on one occasion, and privately she had been of the opinion that Ian was not adjusting to that change with much grace, but gradually she came to appreciate his fierce pride as head of the clan and she was more sympathetic with his irritation.

However, the more she reflected on the disappointing end to their evening, the clearer it became that whatever had upset Ian had begun even before she made her remark about the mythical Jamie MacPherson. Ian had been quiet through supper— preoccupied, she had thought then, with the emotional scene that had preceded the meal. At the time she had been too aroused herself to wonder what he might be thinking as he sat solemnly across from her, but as the days passed she forced herself to face the truth.

What had happened was that Ian had remembered Katrine. It was as simple as that.

She would have done well to remember Katrine herself! If she had, her heart would not be aching now, and she would have more to show for her days than long stretches of pining after Ian and frantic rushings to the door each time an automobile crossed the moor.

She had mistaken physical magnetism for the first sweet stirrings of love, she scolded herself. Ian loved Katrine. What he felt for Jamie was no more than the quickened heartbeat and dry mouth that she herself felt each time her gaze moved over his virile leanness or caught the erotic lift of his mouth's corners. Even when she had despised him for his arrogance and condescension, his maleness had moved her. Her extended stay at the castle had further aggravated the situation. If she could have come straight here . . . if she had not gone picknicking with him and riding across the moor . . . if she hadn't dined with him daily . . .

Angrily, Jamie brought herself up short. What good were all those "if's" now? She had wasted too much of her precious time torturing herself with futile imaginings. Was she such an idiot that she meant to go on wasting more time yearning after a man who had made it quite plain that his only interest in her was an occasional kiss or two?

Ian had enjoyed the few moments of excitement that holding her in his arms had brought, but that was all. He had told her himself that not much of interest broke the routine in these craggy far reaches of Scotland. He had warned her that he and his kinsmen welcomed any diversion. Another woman would have had sense enough to heed so broad a hint.

She should have remembered, too, how long Katrine had been away. Ian was a healthy, physically oriented man. In the absence of his fiancée, he had been attracted to the scent of mimosa . . . to a porcelain-colored skin, delicate as a china teacup. . . .

Jamie's eyes filled with tears, and she shoved aside her polishing rag and the tarnished pewter pitcher she had come across in her uncle's things. She had thought when she made the discovery how handsome the piece would be in the center of her table, filled with golden gorse, but now disillusioned and angry, it seemed to her that no amount of rubbing would bring back the pitcher's glow. It was finished —as she herself was as far as Ian was concerned. Both she and the pewter would best be shoved back up on the shelf.

Jamie had hardly brushed her tears away when the low purr of an approaching automobile broke the silence inside the cottage. With fresh resolve to make better use of her time than she had so far, Jamie kept away from the window, but in a few moments a familiar voice rang out, calling her name.

When Jamie opened the door, Avril stood on the threshold.

"So this is your little hideaway," she said with one of her quick smiles. Without waiting to be asked in, she gave Jamie's swollen eyes a sharp look and came into the middle of the main room.

"It's charming—really," she said after a moment of critical appraisal. "I don't know that I would have used yellow, but—" She shrugged. "It looks just as it should—quaint, simple, and quite utilitarian."

Jamie would have preferred "homey" to "utilitarian," but she held her tongue, admiring instead Avril's crisp flowered voile and wide white garden hat. She looked as though she might be setting out for the queen's tea party, Jamie thought, and then realized with a start that quite obviously Avril had come to share afternoon tea with her.

Hastily, Jamie put the kettle on and then with undisguised pride showed Avril around the tiny cottage. When they came to the new bathroom,

Avril said in an annoyed tone, "Is this what Ian calls 'putting in water'?"

"I couldn't believe it, either," said Jamie. "And it was all done so quickly, too."

"And with such an obvious eye for pleasing you." Then Avril's quick smile appeared again. "But I'm glad for you, dear. It must be terrible enough to be stuck away out here without being deprived in the bargain."

"Stuck away?" Jamie bristled. "It was my choice to come here, you know."

Avril lifted her carefully arched brows. "In all honesty, wouldn't you have preferred staying on at the Hall? Surely Ian invited you to."

Jamie felt her cheeks heating up. "Even if he had, I wouldn't have accepted. I need to be alone to paint."

"You're painting?" Avril glanced around the neat cottage looking for evidence of Jamie's claim.

Jamie flushed. "I usually paint in the morning." The kettle conveniently whistled, and gratefully she hurried toward it. "However, I haven't painted as much as I'd like to. There's been so much to do getting settled."

"And naturally Ian is forever underfoot," said Avril idly, "Ian being very much the laird."

"Actually," said Jamie, keeping her face averted as she filled the tea tray, "I haven't seen him since I moved in."

"Oh." Avril's voice took on a lilting quality. "How thoughtless of Ian. I've come just in time to rescue you, then, from dying of boredom. Alex and I are having a dinner party tomorrow evening, with cards afterward—just a few friends. You must come, of course." She paused. "Ian will call for you."

Jamie broke in quickly. "I'll be delighted to come —but alone, if you don't mind. I imagine I'll want to come back to the cottage early." She forced a light laugh. "I'm a country girl now, you know."

Avril sat down. "What I had in mind was your staying the weekend," she said casually.

"In Applecross?" Jamie showed her surprise. "Oh, I don't think so, but thank you, just the same. I've only just gotten settled here—"

"And you want to paint, I know. Well, don't worry. I promise to leave you entirely to yourself next week, and you can paint to your heart's content then, but you must grant me this one little favor and be my guest for the weekend. Please don't say no. I need you most desperately."

"I don't understand."

"It's Alex. He's invited this tiresome couple—an old school chum and his wife, Charles and Ann Grieve—up from Inverness for golf. I don't golf, you know, and neither does she, and I simply can't bear the thought of those endless hours alone with her. You can help me entertain her, don't you see?"

"Avril—" Jamie could not conceal her amusement. "You of all people would never need help entertaining anyone—least of all, my help. What would I talk about? My London shop job? The croft?"

"Ann might find both charming." Avril sipped her tea, her expression wounded. "I thought we were friends. I counted on you to help me."

Jamie suppressed a sigh. "Well, if you're convinced I can help—"

"Lovely, darling!" Avril granted her one of her most beguiling smiles. "I knew you'd be a brick."

They talked of other things then, but it was plain to Jamie that Avril's mind was elsewhere, and she rose shortly and said her farewells.

"I'll look for you tomorrow evening. Sixish? We'll have drinks before dinner, so do come early. And do allow Ian to call for you, won't you? He'll be staying over, too—golfing with the men. It will please him, I'm sure, to bring you along. You know how lonely he is with Katrine away."

"Let's let him decide, shall we?" Jamie answered stiffly. "He may have other plans."

"What do you mean? That he might be bringing someone else?" Avril laughed. "Don't be ridiculous. He never takes out anyone except Katrine. Well, he takes you out now and then, but that's different, isn't it?" She tilted her head, and with the look of a shrewd, curious bird repeated her question. "Isn't it, darling?"

Jamie fumed around the cottage for an hour after Avril left, scolding herself for behaving like a spine-less idiot. She would never get over her attraction for Ian if she continued to see him, and particularly if she were forced to make the drive into Applecross and back with him in addition to a weekend of dining and games.

However, as the afternoon wore on, she calmed down. Perhaps Avril had done her a favor, after all. If she stayed completely away from Ian, how could she ever be sure she was free of her infatuation? Spending time with him might help her prove to herself that it was possible to fall out of love as easily as it had been to fall in.

But watching the shadows lengthen across the few distant dun-colored slopes that spring had not yet touched, she felt more as if she had fallen into a vat of scalding water than into love. Each time she remembered Ian's embrace, she felt herself flushing. Did he think she had thrown herself at him? Was that why he had withdrawn so hastily into his moody shell?

It was true that her response had been passionate —too much so, she thought now, though at the time she had not thought at all, but simply responded. But if he had taken offense, he should remember that it was he who had aroused that passion. He couldn't expect her to behave like a chunk of wood when his arms were encircling her and his mouth was taking hers.

Again angry tears welled up inside her. All day she had gone around in circles, making resolutions and then casting them to the wind. If Avril hadn't come—if she had gone on with her painting as she had planned, instead of wasting time with that silly pitcher—

But there she was—playing the "if" game again! Thoroughly displeased, Jamie took herself inside, slamming the door against the streamers of purple and gold that were bearing the sun away, and setting out with noisy, impatient gestures the dishes for her simple supper.

Jamie had cleared the kitchen, bathed, and donned a soft melon-colored robe with the intention of settling herself before the fire to study her sketches when the sound of a knock on her door shattered the quiet of the cottage.

The noise startled her—even more, it frightened her. She had heard no car, and for a moment the ridiculous feeling came over her that a ghost of the moor or a loch monster trailing slime might be standing outside her house.

Letting her sketches fall to the table, she called out tremulously, "Who's there?"

A strong voice came back. "Ian."

Torn between relief, excitement and despair, she hurried to turn the key. Ian stood on the threshold, arms folded across his chest. He had on a pair of ancient rubber boots, she saw; also, a tan jacket, worn tweed trousers, and on his head a crumpled gray cap.

He took off the cap as he stepped inside and his eyes moved from the open throat of her robe to the fleece gently molding her breasts and hips. "Have I called too late?"

"No, of course not." Jamie flushed. Her hand brought her collar together. "I took an early bath. I thought I might—" She suddenly recalled the sketches—Ian's portrait among them—that she had left lying on the table. "I had thought I might read for a while," she stammered. His sharp appraisal made her go on. "But I'll be glad for the company."

Unable to meet his searching gaze, she fixed her attention on his boots. Parts of the spongy moor required men to wear them, but so far Jamie had seen them only on crofters. "You must have walked over." She cleared her throat nervously. "No wonder I didn't hear a car. I thought for a minute after your knock came that you might be a ghost."

"I might have been, at that." His steady blue eyes stayed on her face. "They're around, you know."

"Seriously?" Jamie's own eyes widened. Then she remembered that she had not asked him to sit down and led the way toward the fire. Flustered, she scooped up her stack of sketches and shoved them into a space on the other side of her chair. "I recall the night I arrived. Angela mentioned ghosts."

Ian slid deep into the opposite chair and settled himself with perfect assurance. How at home he looked, Jamie thought with a twinge. In his country attire he might have been a simple crofter at the end of a long day's work, instead of the arrogant lord of a baronial mansion. *If he had been, would the way have been smoother between them?* she wondered. "Are there really ghosts in the castle?"

"Three that I know of," Ian announced easily. Then he smiled, and Jamie thought her heart would burst looking at him. "There's a wee old man who frightens all the lady guests on the third floor whenever he passes through their dressing rooms—which I understand were once a part of his quarters. There's Great Aunt Viola, who always appears on Christmas Day wearing a lace hat. And then there is Geraldine."

"Who is Geraldine?"

"According to the family chronicles, she lived in the Hall in the early 1800s, a thwarted physician. Medicine as a profession was out of the question since she was a woman, and a titled one at that, so she had to content herself with studying it rather than practicing." He set his head to one side and said mildly, "I thought perhaps you saw her when you were there."

Jamie tensed. "At Talbert Hall? Where?"

"In the library. Most mornings when the sun is out," Ian went on, "she sits in the tapestried chair by the far window and the sunbeams pass right through her. She makes quite a fascinating picture."

"You're teasing me!"

Ian retained his grave smile. "Not at all. You simply overlooked her when you were there." The corners of his mouth twitched. "It's fortunate you didn't sit on her."

"Ian!" Then they both laughed.

"You must come back one of these mornings and have another look." He paused, gazing at Jamie's flushed face. "The Hall is rather empty without you."

She looked away. "You flatter me."

"If I seem to, that wasn't my intention." His low-pitched voice had the effect of a caress. "Time went faster when you were there."

If time had hung heavy on his hands, why hadn't he come to see her before now? "I imagine," said Jamie stiffly, "that you have quite enough to do without entertaining a full-time guest."

"And you? What have you been doing?" His pointed gaze traveled to the stack of sketches by her chair. "Pursuing your hobby?"

Jamie replied sharply, "Painting is not a hobby for me."

"I see." He bit back a smile. "I beg your pardon."

"I'm not very good yet." Jamie's flush deepened.

"But I take my work far more seriously than I would a mere pastime."

Again he repressed a smile, but he set his head to one side and said solemnly, "Perhaps you would do me the favor of showing me your work."

Jamie caught her breath. "These?" She glared at the stack of sketches as if she hoped they might turn into ashes. "These are only a few I did rather hurriedly."

He put out his hand. "Let me have a look."

"No!"

"Are you ashamed of them?"

"No, I am not! Oh, very well, then, if you insist—" Flushed with embarrassment, she gathered them up from the floor and handed them to him. He settled back into his chair and began slowly to glance through them.

"This one is very fine," he murmured after a minute. "Who is she?"

She! Jamie trembled with relief. "I don't know. An old lady I saw on the street when I passed through Lochcarron."

His brows lifted. "And you remembered her face well enough to put it down later?"

Jamie caught the note of admiration in his voice, and her heart swelled. "I was driving alone. I thought of it a great deal."

"Nevertheless, it's quite a remarkable piece of work." He went back to the sketches in his lap, and in a moment, Jamie—holding her breath—saw him tense. His eyes came up and she felt the full force of his compelling gaze. "This one is of me."

She passed her tongue over her lips, her mouth

too dry to swallow. "Yes. You have an interesting face."

Ian remained silent and went on staring at her.

"Are you displeased because I sketched you?"

"Not displeased. A bit surprised, perhaps."

"I wanted to see if I could catch your expression."

"Do you believe you did?"

Jamie's heart pounded. "Yes."

Without further comment he put the drawing of himself on the bottom of the stack and went on with his study of her other work. There was a scene of one of the glens with a salmon river running through it; another, an action portrait of a fair-haired girl in a kilt-skirt and sweater pedaling her bike; and one more of a bright-looking lad seated on a low stone wall eating strawberries from a bowl.

Ian held that one up. "Do you know who this is?"

Jamie shook her head, still unnerved by Ian's response to her sketch of him. "I saw him the day you took me to tea at Avril's. You left me in the car, you remember—when you went into the tobacconist's shop."

"Did the boy know you were drawing him?"

She shook her head. "I wasn't, actually. I only put down a few lines I thought might be hard to capture later. I used a sheet of paper I found on the floor of the Jeep, by the way. A list of some kind." Jamie ventured a weak smile. "I hope it wasn't something you needed later."

"I hope I'm better organized than that." He smiled suddenly. "The only things I leave lying about are those I want someone else to throw away for me. My more important papers are filed in grand disarray on top of my desk."

Jamie's smile lingered as she recalled the mountain of clutter in his study. "I could probably locate this particular paper if something vital turns up missing. I should have mentioned it before now."

Ian stretched his legs toward the fire. "As a matter of fact, your timing is rather good. With this lad and his berries, you may have saved yourself a hefty sum in repair bills."

"What do you mean?" Jamie's lips parted. "Do you have the bill for the Austin?"

Without comment, Ian produced a sheet of white paper from the pocket of his jacket and then sat back to watch as Jamie paled, reading the figures scratched on it.

"Oh, my," she said when she was finished. "I *am* in trouble."

"I rather thought you might be." Ian took out his pipe and knocked it against the hearth. "But don't worry. I think I may have the solution."

"No, thank you," Jamie said quickly. "You stocked my larder, but I won't allow you to pay for the Austin, too."

"That's not what I had in mind. This boy—" He nodded toward the sketch. "He's William MacPherson's son." With a twinkle he added, "His only son, his pride and joy."

"Who is William MacPherson?"

"Read the heading on your bill."

Jamie's eyes skipped over the print, and then she raised them, bright with eagerness. "Are you saying that Mr. MacPherson might take a portrait of his son as payment for the repair of my car?"

Ian grinned back at her. "I think it's worth a try. Shall I take it with me and have a go at it?"

"Oh, heavens, no!" Jamie snatched the drawing from him. "I'll do a real portrait with oils. No one would give so much as a guinea for this!"

Ian eyed her with amusement. "I think MacPherson would, and far more than that, but I can't blame you for wanting to show him the best you can do. When can you have it ready?"

"By the first of next week, perhaps." Then her expression changed to one of dismay. "No, I can't. I've promised Avril I'd go in to Applecross for the weekend."

Ian sighed. "The jolly old house party. I'd forgotten about it, too. She'll have our heads if we don't show up."

Jamie gave him a surprised stare. "I can't imagine your going anywhere out of intimidation."

"I'm not going because I'm intimidated," he answered sharply, "and certainly not by Avril. It's Alex I feel sorry for—stuck with those dreadful people for two days and nights."

"I don't see why you should pity Alex. They're his friends, not Avril's."

"Who said so?"

"Why, Avril—this afternoon, right there in the chair where you're sitting."

"Then she's made up a story for some reason," said Ian flatly. "Ann and Charles Grieve were customers of Avril's when she was a decorator in Inverness—long before she ever knew Alex. She invites them up two or three times a year to show off her fine house and remind them of how she's come up in the world."

Jamie was speechless.

"Charles Grieve swings a golf club with about as

much finesse as a fly swatter. It's a nightmare to be in a set with him. And on top of that, he's a terrible bore."

"That's what Avril said of his wife," said Jamie, still astonished that Avril had lied to her about something so trivial.

"Well, she's got that much right, at least," Ian said grimly. "I don't envy you if you're left alone with Ann for over five minutes."

"I can't get out of it, I suppose," said Jamie, casting a longing look at the drawing. "I'd much rather work on the portrait."

Ian smiled sympathetically. "If you've accepted, I'm afraid you're stuck. Let that be a lesson to you," he scolded lightly. "Don't let other people lead you around by the nose."

"I never do that," she said, annoyed by his condescension. "Anyway, you're a fine one to talk."

"I'm only going because of Alex." Ian got up, stretching. "I'd better be on my way. I'm getting too comfortable here."

"It's early." Jamie rose, too, her pulse quickening as she watched him glance once more through the drawings. What did he really think of his portrait? Had he seen through her thin story of why she had done it? "I could make a pot of tea."

He put down the drawings and let his gaze slide lazily over her. "I'd rather have a whiskey."

"I'm sorry. I don't have any to offer you."

For a long moment he went on looking at her. "Offer me a kiss, then. You owe me one."

Jamie's violet eyes opened wide. She was aware that color had flooded her cheeks, and she saw from his mocking smile that he had noticed.

"The last time I was here you forgot to kiss me good night," he taunted softly.

On the verge of reminding him that he hadn't stayed long enough to collect it, Jamie bit back the admission and tossed her dark hair. "I don't give kisses to strangers who come walking in out of the night."

He took a step forward and suddenly his arms were wrapped about her in a rough embrace. "I'm no stranger to you," he said thickly.

"Then why do you behave as though you were?" she came back at him, trembling.

"Because you're such a saucy wench." His white teeth flashed in a wicked smile. Then he kissed her full upon the mouth. The electric thrill of his touch coursed through her. *On again, off again!* her brain warned, but her emotions were stronger than memory, and she leaned into his arms, the miserable week she had endured without him dissolving . . . everything dissolving, except the force of his body against hers and the possessive thrust of his lips.

Chapter Six

Mr. and Mrs. Charles Grieve from Inverness were all that Ian had promised they would be—self-important, snobbish and boring. Ann Grieve, a woman of about Alex's age, wore her brown hair drawn back in a tight knot which, instead of the classic look she apparently aspired to, made her narrow face even plainer. Her perfume, heavy and overpowering, hung over the drawing room like a poisonous cloud, and on Saturday afternoon she talked nonstop for an hour about her sister's sinus operation.

As luck would have it, rain fell throughout the day. Alex and Ian, plainly pleased not to be out on the golf course with Charles—who was almost a mirror image of his dull wife, only fifty pounds heavier—set him to talking of how his mansion had once almost been robbed. Like a clock wound up, Grieve ticked off every monotonous detail of the adventure with no care at all that most of his audience had heard it before. Alex went to sleep in his chair soon after Grieve got to the point in his story where he called the police, and Avril beckoned to Ian to come and sit beside her at the piano while she searched through a book for songs for them to sing.

This left Jamie the only listener. Pretending interest, she turned her head mechanically from Charles on the one side to Ann droning on on the other and let her thoughts drift.

How could Avril bear the company of these people as often as Ian claimed she invited them to Applecross? They were wealthy and influential, but so were Alex and Avril, and certainly the Grieves would win them no friends.

But looking at Avril's high color as she sat beside Ian on the piano bench, Jamie decided that of the six of them, Avril was the only one truly enjoying the afternoon. As usual, she was dressed to perfection in a gauzy outfit that set off her blond hair and blue eyes and accented becomingly her vivaciousness. As she leaned closer to Ian's dark thatch, Jamie was struck by the handsome picture they made. Avril, much younger than Alex, was within a few years of Ian's age, and when Jamie saw her hand go out the second time to cover Ian's, it suddenly occurred to Jamie that Avril seemed much too fond of Ian.

A sharp pang of jealousy seized her. Then immediately she rebuked herself. Naturally, Avril was fond of Ian. She hoped to be his sister-in-law. In addition to that, she had worked for months at Talbert Hall while the redecorating was in progress. She must have spent hours consulting with Ian. A strong friendship was bound to have resulted.

However, in Jamie's opinion, there was more than friendship in Avril's attention to Ian as they sat beside each other with the songbook spread out on the piano keys. She watched as beneath the bench

Avril brushed her ankle seductively against Ian's. The glances she gave him were more erotic than platonic, and one would have been hard put to slide even so much as a slip of paper between their shoulders.

It was fortunate, Jamie thought, watching with irritation as Avril pressed herself to Ian's side, that Alex was such a blindly doting husband, or he might have been disturbed by his wife's careless behavior. Then she scolded herself again. Surely Avril would never dare to flirt seriously with Ian when others were present—particularly her husband.

Or would she?

Jamie's breathing stopped. Perhaps Avril had set up the whole weekend with that exact purpose in mind!

Jamie lost entirely the thread of Charles Grieve's narrative as all her senses reacted with shock. When one thought about it, what safer way was there to flirt? No one would dare accuse Avril in her own drawing room in front of her husband. And even if someone did, the more blatant her actions, the more preposterous such an accusation would seem to those watching.

However, no one *was* watching, Jamie realized sourly. Except herself. Grieve had folded his hands over his portly stomach and was addressing the ceiling, and Ann, having bored herself into silence, was leafing through a fashion magazine. Alex slept on, unaware that anyone else was even in the room.

Jamie got out of her chair. "The rain has let up," she announced in a positive voice loud enough to rouse Alex. "I'm going for a walk."

At once Ian left the piano bench. "I'll come along, too. I could use a bit of fresh air."

"We'll all go," said Avril.

Ann Grieve smothered a yawn. "No, thank you. Charles and I never go out when there is water on the streets. One courts arthritis with damp feet, you know. Come over here, Avril, dear. While the others are gone, we can chat, and Alex and Charles can have a nice game of cards."

Jamie saw two angry spots of color leap into Avril's cheeks, and from the doorway she could not resist a parting shot. "You must tell Avril about your sister's surgery, Ann. She was busy at the piano and missed your account. It was performed at Highgate Hospital, Avril," she added with an encouraging smile. "Absolutely fascinating." Then giving her arm to Ian, she moved out of the drawing room into the hall.

Once the door was shut, Jamie pulled apart from Ian and said with annoyance, "If you don't mind, I'll take my walk alone."

Ian gave her an astonished look. "What's wrong with you? Have you swallowed a pickle?"

"I just as well may have. I've spent the afternoon listening to one!"

Ian laughed. "She is dreadful, isn't she? I loved the way you palmed her off on Avril. Avril is so skilled at seeing that everyone else gives Ann an ear, but she never has one for her herself. The last time the Grieves were here, Avril invited a poor young thing from Plockton to share the festivities, and you should have seen how pale and desperate looking she became after only the first evening."

Jamie stood still in the middle of the hall. "Are you always invited when the Grieves visit?"

"Usually."

"Why do you come?"

"For Alex's sake. I told you that."

Jamie brought her chin up. "I think it's because you enjoy flirting with Avril."

A devilish grin broke out on Ian's craggy face. "It's true I'd rather play games at the piano with Avril than be stupefied by Ann. Can you blame me?"

"I think your behavior was disgraceful!"

Ian looked at her angry face, his eyes still amused. "You're certainly on a high horse. I may have to buy you a chocolate soda at Heatherton's Cream Shop to soothe your ruffled feelings."

"It would take more than that to win back my respect," Jamie answered primly. "Avril is married, you know."

Ian's face sobered. Opening the front door, he followed her out onto the sidewalk and then stopped, blocking her way. "Just for the record," he said evenly, "I'm enormously fond of Alex. He's a fine man, and I would never knowingly offend him in any way."

That still doesn't say how you feel about Avril! But Jamie suppressed the retort and drew her lips together in a tight line, glaring until Ian moved aside to allow her to pass.

When she had gone a few steps with Ian following, she turned around and scowled at him. "Haven't I made myself clear? I don't care for your company."

Ian's cool gaze swept over her. "I don't care if you

do or you don't," he answered. "I'm going for a walk, and I'm going with you."

"Even when you're not wanted?"

"Most especially then." Cutting his stride to match her shorter one, he moved along beside her in silence until they reached the heart of the town. Even though the rain had stopped, the sky was still heavily overcast. The commercial fishing fleet was huddled together in the harbor, and slim-winged fulmars circled above. What few people were about strode along briskly in their rain gear, umbrellas opened as if they expected an immediate downpour.

At the end of a long block, Ian slowed and, firmly taking Jamie's elbow, he steered her into a neat little shop with small wrought-iron tables spaced evenly on a gleaming marble floor. It was the ice-cream parlor he had spoken of, and in a moment they were seated, with Ian ordering two chocolate sodas and then folding his arms to stare across at Jamie with a commanding air.

"Now—" he said. "Tell me what's really the matter."

Jamie stared back at him with equal directness. "Nothing."

"I don't believe that—and you don't expect me to."

As always, his compelling gaze disarmed her, and though she would rather have gone on glaring at him defiantly, she said in a low voice, "You irritated me, that's all."

"How? By flirting with Avril?"

"I thought your behavior was disgusting."

"Disgraceful was your first choice, I believe."

"You're bent on infuriating me, aren't you!"

He spread his hands in a gesture of innocence. "On the contrary. I merely want to clear the air, so we can get on with enjoying ourselves. We have the whole rest of the evening, you know, to put up with the Grieves. Hadn't we better spend our reprieve as happily as we can while we have the chance?"

"All right, then, I'll tell you what I think—and if it makes you angry, you can get up and go away afterward, and I won't mind in the least."

She took a breath and plunged forward recklessly despite the condescension she imagined in his crooked smile. "In my opinion, Avril behaved just as disgracefully as you. She was blatantly flirting with you, and I think she did so on purpose to make it seem too open to be believable and thus throw everyone off the truth."

Ian nodded thoughtfully.

"Furthermore," said Jamie, infuriated by his unexpected acquiescence, "I believe she stages these deadly house parties simply for the prolonged pleasure of your company, and that she invited me so that she would have an acceptable excuse to invite you."

"Yes," said Ian with a kindly smile. "I quite agree."

"You agree!" Jamie's violet eyes snapped. "Then you're even more despicable than I thought."

"Why?"

"You say you are fond of Alex, and yet you put your stamp of approval on his wife's betrayal."

"Not at all," he answered. Sighing, he looked about for the waitress and then returned his gaze to Jamie. "Your analysis is perfect, but only up to a point. There are things you don't know, so naturally you can't see the whole picture."

"Then tell me what I don't know," she challenged. "Let's see if it changes my opinion."

"I'll tell you one thing. Alex is a fine fellow, but he's hardly more exciting than the Grieves. One can't blame Avril for wanting a little diversion now and then, can one?"

"I think that's shocking!"

"Oh, don't be so prissy," he answered, finally annoyed. "It's all quite innocent. Besides, Alex is only a part of it—a minor part, at that."

"Then let's hear the major part."

"I'd rather not go into it, if you don't mind. Ah—here we are." He turned his devastating smile on the girl setting a tray on the table, and then lifting his tall soda glass in a kind of salute to Jamie, he said, "I want us to give this our full attention. Here—" He pushed her glass closer. "Drink up. How long has it been since you've had such a treat?"

Jamie ignored the question and the soda, as well. "You're not telling me because there's nothing to tell. You're throwing up a smokescreen."

With an air of pained resignation, Ian set his glass down. "The MacPherson stubbornness." He shook his head. "The clan's glory—and its pitfall. Very well, then. If you insist, I'll state the situation as plainly as I can, and then we'll be done with it." He smiled mockingly at Jamie. "Please pay attention."

Jamie glared. He laughed and then as calmly as if he were remarking on the weather, he said, "I was once in love with Avril's sister, Katrine."

As many times as Jamie had pondered Ian's relationship to Katrine, it had not occurred to her to prepare herself for the moment when he would frankly acknowledge it. She stared at him, speechless.

Ian went on in the same casual tone. "I gave a bit of thought to marrying Katrine, and then I discovered she wasn't the girl for me, and we stopped seeing each other."

He was concocting a lie—and he arrogantly assumed she would believe it! She said flatly, "Naturally, you stopped seeing each other. Katrine is in Edinburgh."

"Edinburgh isn't the end of the earth," he answered. "I can go there when I choose—and I did when I had a reason for going."

Jamie felt as if she were smothering. "I don't see what that has to do with Avril and you."

"Everything," said Ian with clipped assurance. "Avril was vexed when Katrine and I went our separate ways. Or perhaps 'distraught' is a better word. Since then she's all but stood on her head to bring us back together."

"By giving house parties when Katrine is miles away in medical school?"

"Exactly." He drew on his straw with obvious pleasure. "It seems roundabout, I know, but that's the way it is. And more than that—you're the bait."

"What?"

"So was that poor girl from Plockton," he said complacently, "and another from farther up the coast at Christmastime. It's really quite amusing how Avril chooses my dinner partners from the most unlikely candidates she can find."

Jamie's face turned scarlet, but Ian, busily spooning ice cream, went on arrogantly. "She closets me

with them for the weekend—in her presence, of
course, so that she can keep an eye on me, thereby
hoping to keep me free from any real entanglements
until she can persuade Katrine to resume our romance."

"You're saying that it was Katrine who ended it?"
Jamie was aware of how brutal her question was, but
her own pain was too great for her to care.

A dark flush spread across Ian's throat. "It was
not entirely Katrine's doing."

"Well, it really doesn't matter whose it was, does
it?" Jamie pushed back her chair and stood up, her
face scarlet. "I don't believe anything you've told
me, anyway. But that doesn't matter, either, because I don't care who you're in love with." Her chin
trembled. "You can carry on in whatever way you
choose with Avril or Katrine or whoever—just don't
bore me with the details."

Ian caught up with Jamie at the far end of the long
block. "I can run three miles without so much as a
stitch in my side," he announced when he drew
abreast of her. "Just set the pace."

Then he saw that her cheeks were wet with tears,
and he put out his arm and stopped her abruptly,
swinging her around to face him in the deserted
street.

"What is it? Why are you so upset?" But his
penetrating gaze only brought a fresh flood of tears,
and wrapping his arm around her shoulder, he
moved on down the street with her pressed to his
side until they came to a boardwalk leading to the
water and a sheltered spot where the wind would not
reach them.

"Here, now." He took out a handkerchief and wiped her tears away, smiling a little at her stricken look and unromantic hiccupping.

"What did I say that hurt you so?" he inquired quietly.

Jamie pressed the handkerchief to her eyes. "Don't talk about it. I've made a terrible fool of myself. You'll make me feel worse if you keep on."

Tenderly, he lifted her chin. "I don't want to make you feel worse, but I do want to get to the bottom of this. Was it my saying I was once in love with Katrine?"

"Why should I care about that?" she answered hotly.

"Why, indeed?" He spent a long moment looking at her. "What was it, then? Was it what I said about your being an unlikely candidate for my affections?"

"I'm no candidate at all for your affections!"

"Would you like to be?"

She would have struck him, but just in time he caught her hand and brought it firmly into his lap. "I was only testing the water." He smiled wickedly. "Not making the ultimate pronouncement." He persisted, peering intently at her. "It *was* what I said about Avril's choosing my partners, wasn't it? Tactless, of course, but see here—you're overlooking the most important point. I was explaining what Avril thinks, not what I think." Jamie's guarded expression told him he had struck the heart of their discord, and he went on soothingly.

"Avril knows that too much independence in a woman irks me because that was part of the trouble between Katrine and me. She knows that the kind of spirited sauciness you carry off so well"—he grinned again—"frequently upsets me. She knows you and I are constantly quarreling." His eyes glowed warmly on Jamie. "Now, taking all that together, won't you admit that you win the prize for being the least likely candidate—in Avril's eyes, at least—to impress me?"

Jamie's mouth tightened. "I'll never admit to anything you try to trick me into saying—and I've never tried to impress you."

"Ah—that's the ticket." Visibly cheered by her show of irritation, Ian put his arm around her again and squeezed her shoulders in a comradely fashion. "You're getting back to yourself, and that's a relief. I hardly know you when you're all teary and soppy."

Jamie winced. Two things were becoming clearer by the moment. One was that her feelings for Ian went even deeper than she had realized. And the other was that Ian's feelings for her were no more or less than when he had stuck his bearded head into her Austin and asked if she were stalled.

No matter how tenderly he had treated her while she was weeping, he was still in love with Katrine. He had made up that cock-and-bull story about breaking up with her because he was too proud to admit that Katrine was more interested in medicine than in him. Jamie knew the truth from Avril, but unaware that she did, Ian was able to sit there quite pleased with his arm around her because he thought he had saved face.

In spite of her anger, Jamie's heart went out to him. *His dear, wonderful face.* Her fingers yearned to caress his craggy profile. She had come perilously close in the ice-cream parlor to revealing how much she cared for him. That must never happen again, not if she were to preserve even a shred of pride. She drew a long, unsteady breath. "I'd like to go home, please."

Ian smiled sympathetically. "To the cottage, you mean."

"Certainly not." She forced a scornful note into her voice. "Back to Avril's. In case you've forgotten, we're expected for dinner."

Ian answered brusquely. "Oh, forget that. I think we've had it with house parties this go-around, don't you?" He brought his lips to within inches of hers. "Let's go for a drive. There's an inn I know on the Gairloch Peninsula. We can have dinner there and take a starlit ride home across the moors. Wouldn't you prefer that to more of Ann Grieve?"

"There aren't going to be any stars," said Jamie, made almost faint by his nearness.

"You're wrong," he murmured. "There are some now—in your eyes." His other arm brought her closer, and his head came down. In the split-second before his mouth covered hers, Jamie saw over his shoulder a white face pressed against the back window of a long black car passing slowly in the street. Then she lost herself in Ian's kiss.

Jamie and Ian lingered in their sheltered spot near the harbor. Ian's kiss lit new fires of passion in them both, and Jamie, in spite of her resolves, melted twice more into his arms before prudence and the curious glances of passersby sent her to the other end of the bench. But she had come under his spell again and longed to accept his invitation to dinner. However, her sense of the fitness of things made her hesitate.

"How can we just walk out on Avril without some valid excuse?" she argued.

"We'll tell her we're going home," said Ian flatly. "You have work to do. That's true, isn't it? You want to get to work on the portrait."

"But we're not going home."

"She won't know that. Anyway, we'll eventually arrive back at the cottage. We're not required to present Avril with a timetable, you know."

He kissed her once more, and finally Jamie gave in. "But you must be the one to make our excuses."

"Gladly," said Ian. But when they arrived back at the Stuart mansion there was a telephone call waiting for Ian, and by the time he had finished with it and made another which the first required, the butler was already announcing dinner and Avril was waiting on Charles Grieve's arm to lead the way into the dining room.

"I'm sorry," murmured Ian as he escorted Jamie in. "It appears our escape has been foiled—for tonight, at least. But we'll get an early start in the morning and be at the inn in time for lunch. How is that?"

Jamie was nodding her assent when she caught their hostess's icy stare on them, and she slipped into her chair without answering. Was it Avril who had peered at them from the car when they were kissing? Jamie shivered, looking at Avril's stony countenance.

But perhaps it was best if Avril had seen them. Ian was a free agent. And so was she. If they chose to kiss each other, it was no one's business but their own. Katrine would have to fight her own battle if she cared enough for Ian to bother—or if Avril were annoyed on her own account, it was a good enough lesson for her after behaving so outrageously in front of her own husband.

Cheered by her little pep talk to herself, Jamie gave her full attention to Avril's excellent meal. Poached salmon fringed with parsley and watercress filled one fine china platter, and delicately diced turnips from the Stuarts' kitchen garden were on another. Mounds of queenies—those small, delicious loch clams gathered by young divers—made another tempting dish, and several salads completed the spread. One of Avril's numerous liveried servants poured a hearty red wine, and Avril, despite her initial look of displeasure, seemed to have regained her high spirits as she chatted gaily with her friends.

Watching her at the end of the table in the brilliant red gown she had changed into for dinner, Jamie felt herself a dowdy guest still clad in the wool dress she had worn all day.

Poor Avril, she thought, feeling suddenly remorseful as she remembered Ian's remark about Alex. Although Avril's life appeared to be exactly what she wanted—full of glitter and prestige and an abundance of material possessions—she must at times feel stifled in the sterile atmosphere of her mansion with a husband who was nearly thirty years her senior and whose principal topic of conversation was herself. No wonder she craved Ian's attentions.

Jamie stole a look at Ian across the table, and her pulse quickened when he returned the look with an intimate smile that reminded her of his caresses and of the tender way he had held her and of his fiery lips on hers.

After what had passed between them in the afternoon, Jamie no longer believed that Ian was in love with Katrine. No man could be in love with one woman and kiss another as Ian had kissed her. He was a proud man and might still be touchy about his break-up with Katrine, but she was convinced he did not seriously care for Avril's sister.

He had given no firm indication that he was in love with her, either, she cautioned herself, but she was confident of the strong attraction between them—and who could tell, she thought with a thrill, what tomorrow might bring?

The prospect of traveling with Ian in the morning set up a warm glow within Jamie, and for the rest of the meal she felt as lighthearted and giddy as Avril also seemed to be feeling. Even dreary Ann Grieve became infected by their gaiety, and Charles, hearing his wife's laughter, put on a brighter face himself.

The meal was by far the most pleasant hour the six of them had spent together, and by the time it had ended Jamie found herself actually glad that she and Ian had not slipped away as they had originally planned. Avril had her faults, but she was a conscientious hostess, and if her guests did not prove to be particularly agreeable, at least she deserved a show of appreciation for the excellent food and gracious surroundings she had provided.

After dinner Jamie was content to adjourn with the others to the drawing room, where Avril, at the piano, played the songs she and Ian had selected in the afternoon, and everyone else gathered around to sing. Surprisingly, Ann Grieve had a rather sweet voice for so sour a countenance, and they let her carry the soprano parts, while Jamie and Avril harmonized on the alto and the men provided the bass. They rounded out the evening by examining Alex's collection of early photographs of the region, which Jamie found particularly fascinating. At eleven everyone said good night.

Climbing the stairs between Alex and Ian, Jamie looked forward to slipping between the crisp linen sheets in her bedroom and reliving in the darkness every precious moment she had spent with Ian. When he squeezed her hand and offered husky wishes for pleasant dreams, she smiled to herself, certain she would have them.

Chapter Seven

The dinner party had been over for nearly an hour, and Jamie was just out of her bath and climbing into bed when a knock stopped her.

At the door she discovered Avril.

Despite her dismay, Jamie put on a bright smile and stood aside to welcome her visitor. Slender and imperious, Avril brushed past her. From the center of the room she said in a tight voice, "May I sit down for a moment?"

"Of course." Jamie pushed forward a chair and took a seat herself on the tufted stool in front of the dressing table. "It was a delightful evening, Avril. I had no idea Ann had such a lovely—"

"It's this afternoon I've come to talk about," Avril broke in.

Jamie's heart flew up in her throat. So the face peering from the Rolls-Royce had belonged to Avril, after all! Then she saw the strange excitement that had taken over Avril's countenance, and she realized that the purpose of her visit had yet to be explained. "What is it? What's happened?"

"I've had a letter," Avril exclaimed breathlessly. "I looked for you to share it earlier, but you were still out with Ian. When you returned there wasn't time, and I've been on pins and needles all evening waiting for a chance to tell you." Her blue eyes burned with a feverish brightness. "But I'm glad I waited. This is so much cozier, so much the better moment. We can read it together."

"A letter?" Jamie stared blankly at her. "From whom?"

"From Katrine, of course." Avril's announcement rang out in the silence, followed by delighted laughter. "Oh, you can't imagine how it changes everything! *Everything,* my dear! All my hopes, my dreams—they're coming true at last. But here—" She thrust her hand into the pocket of her robe and brought forth a pale blue envelope. "Read it for yourself."

Jamie drew back, as if the touch of the envelope had scalded her. "I couldn't read your letter."

Avril frowned. "Why ever not?"

"Because it wasn't written to me."

"I'm inviting you to read it." An edge came into Avril's voice, though her smile stayed bright. "I insist."

"Katrine wouldn't approve, I'm sure."

With pronounced patience Avril said, "What Katrine has written, everyone in Applecross will soon know. But you've been such a comfort to me, allowing me to confide my anxieties about Katrine and Ian, that I couldn't bear it if you didn't share my joy now." She leaned across the space between them and pressed the letter into Jamie's hand. "Read it at once. Then we can rejoice together."

"Really, Avril—"

"Read it!"

With trembling fingers, Jamie slipped the pale

paper from its envelope. Steadying it on the dresser top, she read the slanting line of greeting. *My dearest darling sister.* She shrank from the harsh black letters that seemed to jump from the page. She had not pictured Katrine as a person who would write with such decisive sweeping force. Glancing swiftly down the page, she saw Ian's name . . . the word "love" . . . the word "marriage." Blindly, she shoved the letter back at Avril. "I'm sorry. I feel as though I were violating a confidence."

"Nonsense." Avril's smile hardened. "I'll read it to you, then. You can't object to that, surely." Without waiting for Jamie's assent, she began in a voice charged with excitement. *"My dearest darling sister, as you know, for months I have refused to see Ian, refused to take his constant calls or to answer his daily letters. I couldn't bear to give up medicine, and I felt he had no right to insist that I do so. But a miracle has happened, my darling sister. After all these months of hiding behind my books, I have discovered that what I actually cannot bear to give up is Ian. I love him too deeply. It's as simple as that. Marriage to him, I have finally realized, is the only state in which I can ever find true happiness!"*

Avril's eyes flicked up and took in Jamie's blanched countenance. With a smile, she continued reading. *"I know that there will be times when I will pine for my lost career, but for Ian the sacrifice is worth it. Geraldine and I will simply have to bear each other up on those days when I long for my cadavers and formaldehyde."* Avril's eyes came up again, gleaming in the reflected lamplight. "She makes a little joke there, Jamie. Geraldine is—"

"I know who Geraldine is," Jamie interrupted woodenly.

Avril pressed the letter to her breast. "Isn't it wonderful? Isn't it marvelous! I've read these lines a dozen times, and I still can't believe it. Oh, Jamie, can you realize how thrilled I am?"

Jamie passed her tongue over parched lips. "Does Ian know?"

"He soon will." Avril scanned the letter again. "Yes—here it is. Katrine says, *'I've just finished writing to Ian and pouring out my love. Your letters go out in the same post.'*"

"His letter is waiting at Talbert Hall, then," said Jamie faintly.

Avril nodded. "Can you imagine how difficult it was for me to keep silent this evening? If I had told him, the dear boy would have left for Edinburgh at once, and he may want to murder me for *not* telling him when he discovers he's wasted a whole day and night with us when he might have been with Katrine. But of course I mustn't spoil Katrine's surprise. She would never forgive me."

"No—" Jamie stared sightlessly at Avril's smiling face. "I'm sure she never would."

"Why, darling!" Avril set her head to one side and said in a teasing voice, "You're quite as stunned as I, aren't you? It's amazing that in such a short time you could have become so wrapped up in all our lives that you can actually feel as keenly about this as I do." Her silken voice covered the silence that hung between them. "You do feel keenly, don't you, darling?"

Jamie managed somehow to get to her feet. "Forgive me, Avril. I'm very tired. I'm afraid at the moment I don't feel much of anything. But I can understand your excitement. I know how much Katrine's happiness means to you."

"And Ian's happiness." Avril looked pointedly at Jamie. "Katrine is quite a lucky girl, wouldn't you agree?"

"Please excuse me, Avril. I'm really too exhausted even to think."

"I quite understand." Avril rose, her clinging robe outlining in a becoming fashion her slim hips and full breasts, but in her eyes an animal brightness burned. "Sleep well, my dear. But I'm sure you will—with such delightful news to dream upon."

As soon as the door closed behind Avril, Jamie snatched up the letter from the dresser top. Swiftly, her eyes moved over the sharply slanting letters. *I love him. . . . What I cannot bear to give up is Ian. . . .*

Her heart pounding, Jamie lowered the page.

"But perhaps Ian can bear to give *you* up, Katrine," she said aloud, taking courage from the sound of her own voice. While Katrine was placidly making up her mind, Ian's life had moved on without her.

I entered it! Jamie thought, her blood beginning to flow again. This letter could not alter what had happened that afternoon. Nor could it change the way Ian had kissed her and held her in his arms. Whatever Ian and Katrine had shared, it was over. Avril had continued to breathe upon the ashes, and it seemed now that she had stirred a spark at last, but if Ian felt as Jamie believed he must, it would be quickly extinguished.

Turning off the lamp, she slid between the sheets and pulled the covers to her chin. Time would tell. Tomorrow when Ian opened his letter from Katrine, she would know his true feelings.

But before that, there was the promised trip in the morning to the Gairloch Peninsula. She and Ian would be together for hours. There would be moments in his arms again. If she were right, if Ian felt as she believed he was beginning to, there was nothing in Katrine's letter that would matter in the slightest.

Rolling along through the wild and magnificent wilderness north of Applecross, Jamie felt herself wrapped in a secure cloak of contentment. Before seven o'clock a knock had awakened her, and when she opened the door, still flushed from dreaming, Ian had stood there ready with a kiss that began tenderly but within moments had locked them into a heated embrace. Only Jamie's frail gown and peignoir and the rough cloth of Ian's jacket had separated flesh from flesh. When they parted at last, their eyes were bright with suspended ardor and their breathing weighted with arousal.

"Be ready in half an hour," Ian had whispered. "I've already alerted the host, and I'm off to make our heartfelt excuses to the hostess."

"She won't be up," said Jamie, reluctant to let him go.

"Then I'll get her up," he answered with devilish glee and disappeared toward Avril's apartment. In a few minutes he was back with an impatient request through the door that Jamie hurry.

"Avril was surprisingly affable when I broke the

news of our departure," said Ian, reaching out to draw Jamie closer on the seat beside him. "She seemed positively delighted that we were leaving, in fact." He brought his brows together with a look of mock despair. "Do you suppose we could have worn out our welcome?"

"Possibly," Jamie answered absently, wondering as she had a dozen times already how he would react when he read Katrine's letter.

She glanced gratefully at the pale summit of Beinn Eighe rising on their left and breathed a prayer of thanksgiving that the silver Ferrari was going in the opposite direction from Talbert Hall. Ian had decided during the night that they must take the ferry across Loch Maree—the loveliest of the Highland lakes, in his opinion—and spend an hour or so on the island, in its center, called Eilean Maree.

He spoke of it again now. "You'll love the island. It's one of my favorite spots, and it's been too long since I've been there."

Had the last time been with Katrine? But Jamie shook off the resentment that thoughts of Katrine always brought and turned a smiling face to Ian. "What does the name mean?"

He put his arm across her shoulder and brushed his lips to her cheek. "Eilean means 'island,' of course, and Maree is a corruption of Saint Maelrubba, the legendary holy man who made his home there."

"What are its main attractions?"

"Won't I spoil it for you if I tell you?"

"I think I'll enjoy it twice as much. I'll know what to look forward to."

Ian went on then to describe some of the island's charms, dwelling in particular on the peaceful, brooding quiet of its oak and holly forests. "Quite a contrast to the pagan rites that raged there for years," he concluded.

Jamie voiced her surprise. "Wasn't the saint—whatever you called him—a Christian?"

"Maelrubba," Ian supplied. "Yes, he was. As a matter of fact, it was he who founded the Church of Applecross. His grave is there in the churchyard. Unfortunately, however, old beliefs struck deep in the islanders. In spite of their respect for the holy man, bulls were sacrificed there well into the late 1600s, and even more recently than that the waters of a sacred well were alleged to cure insanity."

"Shall we sprinkle a few drops from it on ourselves?" Jamie teased. "Just in case?"

Ian shared her amusement. "We're too late, I'm afraid. I understand that after the treatment was tried on a mad dog, the well dried up in protest. However, what remains surrounding it is more interesting, in my opinion."

Jamie pressed him for details, but it was not until they were on the island itself that she discovered the phenomenon to which Ian had referred.

Close by the shallow depression that marked the old well site, a cluster of oak trees showed forth, thicker than their bark, thousands of coins that through the years had been hammered edgewise into their trunks for much the same reason that superstitious folk in other lands toss pennies into fountains. The copper from the coins had poisoned the trees and all were dead or dying, but nevertheless, Ian took a stone and pounded in a penny for himself and one for Jamie, pausing afterward to join hands with her around the trunk so that they could make their own wishes.

Their eyes met as Jamie silently breathed hers, and she wondered what longing it was that filled Ian's gaze with such intensity. Was he dreaming, as she was, that love would grow between them? That this brief visit to Eilean Maree would not be the last one they would share?

Whatever his unspoken wish had been, when they were walking again toward the ferry that had brought them across the sky-blue lake, Ian drew her into the shadows created by a grove of holly, and clasping his arms around her waist, he brought her close against his body. When they kissed, his lips explored hers with a new ardor, his passion tightly leashed, but making itself known in the pressure of his hands sliding down her hips and back again to encircle her waist, and the endearments whispered against her cheek.

Afterward, they crossed the lake, and then dawdled for a time beside a broad bay further up the shore where glowing pink sand formed a fine beach. While they lunched from a vendor's cart, Ian told Jamie of having come there as a boy with his grandfather to watch the herring fleet make port. That tale led to another, with Jamie eagerly drinking in every detail of the MacPherson family history. When they finally entered the cozy lounge of an ancient hotel at the end of the peninsula, it was tea time. They glanced about at the crowd that had already gathered and then chose the even cozier pub next door for glasses of champagne.

Driving home under the starlit sky that Ian swore he had produced with his money-tree wish, Jamie snuggled contentedly against his side. "It was a perfectly wonderful day," she told him drowsily.

His lips brushed her temple. "I've never known a happier one."

Joy swelled within her. *Not even with Katrine?* she longed to say, but asked instead if he would come back to the croft with her to have supper. The trip to Eilean Maree had made them too late for lunch at the inn and too early for dinner. "I'm sure I can scrape something together," she said.

"What?" he mocked. "Boiling soup and cheese again? Not on your life. While you were sketching the harbor in Gairloch, my dear, I was telephoning the Hall. If the cook has followed my instructions, we'll have a fine bait of haggis and turnips waiting for us, and more brown beer, too, if you can manage it after all the champagne you downed back there instead of tea."

"That was your idea!" said Jamie indignantly. "I'd have been quite content with joining those very proper ladies and gentlemen by the fireside if you had allowed it."

"The pub was nicer, don't you think?" he teased. "That shadowy little table where the barmaid couldn't see us."

"I must ask you, laird of Talbert Hall, to be more selective of your sites if you intend to continue kissing me in the daylight," Jamie answered, pretending disdain.

In answer, Ian pulled over to the side of the road and took her into his arms. "I intend to keep kissing you in the daylight and in the dark and whenever else I please, for as long as I please," he murmured thickly. "Is that clearly understood?"

Jamie's lips moved under his. "Don't I have anything to say about it?"

"You can say yes." He bit her lip lightly. "Say it," he said hoarsely.

They stopped twice more before they reached Talbert Hall—once to kiss again and to hold each other closely, and once more when the moon appeared, shedding a mystical white veil over the gaunt mountains and haunting glens.

It was far past dinner time when they reached Talbert Hall. The closer they came to the formidable mansion guarding its own craggy peak, the more nervous Jamie became. All day she had felt as calm and assured as if her future with Ian were a settled fact, but there was one more bridge to cross, and suddenly she was terrified of it.

Ian noticed her edginess, and putting it down to hunger, he assured her that if haggis and turnips were not to her taste, there were certain to be other delectables to suit her palate. She covered her anxiety by quickly agreeing that she was indeed starving and looking forward to the treat he had ordered.

The tall white-haired butler, Robert, whom Jamie had grown so fond of during her week at the Hall, let them in, and Jamie climbed the stairs to freshen up before their meal was served. Ian went directly to his study.

She lingered for a few minutes in front of the

dresser in her old room, staring at her pale reflection and wishing that the moment when her eyes met Ian's again was over.

What if she were wrong? What if when Ian read Katrine's letter all his former feelings for her returned? It was true that between herself and Ian there existed a strong bond of physical attraction and a joyous appreciation of life that made their moments together wonderfully special, but she had no way of knowing what Katrine and Ian had shared. They had known each other for years . . . had spent countless days together—not just one on a magic island in the middle of a blue loch. . . .

Fighting down her panic, Jamie crossed the room and went down the stone stairs, head high, cheeks bright. *Let it be finished quickly,* she prayed while her fingernails bit into the cold palms of her hands.

Ian was pacing in front of the fire in the small drawing room. When he heard Jamie's step he whirled, and she saw how animated his expression was, how aglow his eyes. He smiled broadly.

It must be all right, she thought in numb relief.

Then he spoke in a voice filled with impatience. "Something's come up, Jamie—an unbelievable bit of luck. I won't take time to explain, but I have to go to Edinburgh tonight. Now, in fact. Immediately. Dallying around all day, I may have missed the opportunity of a lifetime, but let's hope not."

Jamie stared at him. "You're going to Edinburgh?"

He spoke again in a voice edged with irritation. "That's what I'm saying. Yes. I'm going at once.

Dinner has been laid for you in the dining room. Spend the night here if you like—or take the Jeep and go on to the cottage."

He crossed the room quickly and Jamie saw that he meant to kiss her. All her senses cried out for his touch, but some latent bit of pride rose in her at the last moment before his lips came down, and she stepped aside, turning her face away. Resentment bitter as gall filled her. She wanted no crumbs from Katrine's table.

Ian's look of injured surprise turned quickly into a hostile glare. And then without a word he was gone.

Chapter Eight

The days crawled by for Jamie after she returned to the croft following Ian's departure for Edinburgh.

Each morning when she dragged herself from her bed she reminded herself how lucky she was to be rising in her own cottage with nothing to do all day except paint, but the ambition that had drawn her to the Highlands had lost its meaning.

Her work was going well enough, but she cared little for it and could think only of the exhilaration Ian's embrace had stirred and of the shattered dreams that haunted her. With burning regret, her thoughts returned again and again to that enchanted day on the Gairloch Peninsula, when she had spun those fragile castles in the air that Ian's hastening away to join Katrine had dashed to bits. Now even reality itself seemed like a pointless dream.

Nevertheless, she worked doggedly, concentrating most of her efforts on the portrait of the mechanic's young son, which she hoped to have ready to take into Applecross by the end of the week.

But late on Friday, standing at the kitchen sink cleaning her brushes, she glanced up and saw Ian's silver Ferrari coming over the moor.

Her heart stopped. *When had he come home? Had he brought Katrine with him? Why was he coming here?* She clung to the edge of the sink, watching the car's progress. Perhaps he was on his way to another croft farther down the road. But then she saw the Ferrari slow and turn in at her own lane, and hastily she rinsed her hands and shoved back a loose lock of hair from her forehead. With dismay, she glanced down at her paint-spattered smock and shoes, muddy from the trek she had made earlier to sketch by the river.

What did they have to say to each other? Had he come to tell her that he and Katrine were to be married? What could she answer to that?

She was still standing paralyzed by the sink when Ian's knock came. Trembling, she chose to stay where she was and called out faintly for him to come in.

In his absence she had renounced him for his faithlessness, for his cruel treatment of her, for leading her on when he cared nothing for her—but the moment his familiar frame stood outlined in the doorway, she could think of nothing except the joy that flooded her.

"Ian—" Eagerly, she stepped forward. Then recalling her bedraggled appearance, she hesitated, running a hand nervously down the folds of the smock. "When did you come home?"

"An hour ago." He stopped inside the doorway, his lips parted and an unreadable expression shrouding his countenance. "How are you?"

The truth sprang to her lips, but she stifled it with a stiff reply. "I couldn't be better, thank you. How was Edinburgh?"

"A jungle."

His blunt reply goaded her into another question. "Did you see Katrine?"

His dark brows jumped together. "Why do you ask?"

"Why shouldn't I ask?"

Ian glared. "If it's so important for you to know, why don't you hire a detective?"

Seething, Jamie searched for a suitable response, but before she could think of one, his glowering gaze took in her clothing and he said with pointed sarcasm, "What have you been doing in that rig? Cutting peat?"

Jamie flushed scarlet. "If it's any of your business, I've been painting. I wasn't expecting visitors."

"Then I won't stay."

"Stay or go as you like," she flared. "It certainly makes no difference to me."

"Still sulking, I see," he flung back at her.

"I have no idea what you mean."

His lip curled. "Sulking. It's what you were doing when I left, and it's obvious you've used the time between to perfect your mood."

Jamie's spine stiffened. "What I was doing when you left was standing alone in your drawing room, having just been informed by the man who had invited me to dinner that he suddenly had better things to do than share it with me."

Ian smiled sardonically. "Sulking. Just as I said."

"Did you drive all the way across the moor to pick a fight with me?"

"I don't care particularly whom I fight with. I suppose you'll do as well as anyone."

Jamie recoiled. Was this arrogant male standing in

her doorway hurling insults at her the same man she had been pining for for days? Then suddenly she understood. Katrine had remained in Edinburgh to finish her work, and Ian—forced to come home without his fiancée—was angry at the world. The last trace of the joy she had felt at seeing him vanished.

"Why did you come here?" she said flatly.

"I wonder myself," he muttered. Then fixing his gaze on the pulse that jumped erratically in her throat, he said coldly, "My original intention was to make sure you were all right."

His words stung like a wasp. "Of course I'm all right. Did you think just because you went away that I couldn't go on living?"

The acid rebuke startled him. "It occurred to me that you might need something."

"I certainly don't need you!"

The insult set his eyes ablaze. "You're an even bigger baby than I thought. Still swelled up like a toad because I didn't sit down to dinner with you. Look here—" He took a step toward her, his rangy body casting a threatening shadow across the stone floor of the cottage. "I don't know what you expect of a man—though I hardly think one could label the milquetoast that you'd have at your beck and call a man. But I can tell you what you can expect of me. First and foremost, I am in charge of my own life. I do as I see fit, when I see fit, and in whatever manner I choose. No one else dictates my priorities. When that telegram came for me to come to Edinburgh—"

"Letter!" said Jamie.

The contradiction made with such certainty enraged him. "I said telegram, blast it, and I mean telegram!"

Jamie was perilously close to tears. "Whatever it was, you dropped everything and ran as if your life depended on getting to Edinburgh in the next five minutes no matter how anyone else felt about it. That's enough for me!"

"That's more than enough for you." His furious gaze seared her. "You always put yourself first, don't you? Well, I'll tell you something. Some circumstances are more important than one individual wanting her own way. That these particular ones might not have warranted my haste is beside the point."

He turned on his heel then and stalked out of the cottage, heat radiating from him as he flung open the door of the Ferrari and slammed it after him.

Jamie stood where she was, clutching her fistful of paintbrushes until the sounds of the car's motor grew too faint to distinguish it from the calls of the gray crows swooping down over the glen, and then she leaned against the counter and gave herself to wracking sobs.

Days went by, and at least once an hour Jamie imagined she heard Ian returning and rushed to the door . . . or she thought she heard his voice . . . or she forced herself to go on with her work instead of getting into the Austin and driving to Talbert Hall to confront him.

He had no right to barge in on her the way he had done, slinging insults at her and acting in general like a beast just broken out of a cage. It wasn't her fault that he was miserable because he had left Katrine behind. If he felt so devastated at being away from her, he should have stayed in Edinburgh and not come back to take out his unhappiness on someone fully as unhappy as he.

But no matter how she ranted, her heart ached for him—and for herself, and for the precious moments they had shared that had come to nothing. What a fool she had been to spend her love on a man who by his own admission was irritated by her. She should have realized that even without Katrine's interference the erotic energy that always ignited them would eventually burn itself out. Ian would never yoke himself for long to a woman with independent ideas.

Katrine was independent, she thought bitterly, *but obviously Katrine was cleverer than herself.* She had not even needed to write the letter she had mentioned to Avril, but had simply sent a telegram, and Ian had dropped everything and gone running to her. Desolate, Jamie wondered what one could say in a telegram beyond *I love you* to heal a quarrel. Perhaps that was enough. *I love you.* She had never spoken those words to Ian, though she had longed to in the few minutes before they arrived at Talbert Hall the night he went away to Edinburgh. *If she had, would it have made any difference?*

Probably not, she acknowledged sadly. The moment he heard from Katrine, the wonderful day they had spent together had passed out of his mind as if it had never existed. All he remembered of it was that Jamie had turned away from his farewell kiss—and even *that* he had misunderstood.

At the end of the week as Jamie was preparing to take the portrait of William MacPherson's son to Applecross, she forced herself to face the facts. Ian would never belong to her. *Forget him,* she told her mirror image sternly. *Forget the touch of his lips. Forget his hands on your body. Forget that you were once fool enough to imagine living with him at Talbert Hall for the rest of your life.*

Bending her tear-streaked cheeks to the basin full of water, she scrubbed with furious energy, as if her efforts might penetrate her skin and cleanse her of her yearnings. But when she raised her face to towel it dry, the hollowness inside her persisted. It claimed all her thoughts while she dressed, and was still with her when she set out after lunch across the moor with the portrait wrapped in a sweater on the seat beside her.

The last vestiges of winter had disappeared during the week, and riding along, Jamie opened the window and let the warm, fragrant air of the uplands blow into the car. *No more fires,* she told herself, *no more coats—and no more wintry thoughts, either.* Even so, as the Austin passed Talbert Hall she could not refrain from searching the grounds for some sign of Ian. She found none, though his two dogs were asleep on the wide stone steps and the Jeep was parked in the driveway.

With nostalgia, Jamie thought of the lovely garden enclosed behind the wall. She imagined that pansy faces bordered the walks by now and stalks of delphinium and columbine swayed in the spring breezes. Her heart lurched. Perhaps by now Katrine was there, too, sitting in the garden with Ian, planning their wedding.

Jamie turned her eyes back to the road, but all the way into Applecross she pictured Ian with his arms about the hazy creature who in her mind was Katrine. She saw them walking, whispering together in the drawing room, sending adoring glances at each other across the dinner table. What kind of wife would Katrine be? If she herself had married Ian, she would have hoped to fill the castle with children —dark-haired lads in kilts, and sunny-faced lassies wearing white aprons and plaid bows in their hair and shiny patent-leather shoes on their feet. But perhaps Katrine would not wish to be bothered by children. Jamie could not imagine Ian anything but lonely if that were the case.

Despite her earlier resolves, the thought of Ian being lonely pierced her with despair, and she was glad when the white cottages of the fishing village at last came into view.

Within a few minutes she had located William MacPherson's garage, which adjoined his house, and presented herself and the portrait in nervous trepidation, but she quickly discovered that she had no cause for concern.

The jovial mechanic was overwhelmed by the sight of his son and heir peering mischievously at him over a bowl of painted strawberries and straightway summoned his wife, who just as quickly called the boy. The three of them were enchanted by the portrait, and before the interview was over, three neighbors had been called in for expressions of admiration, and the entire bill for Austin's repair was forgiven.

Striding along the sidewalk afterward, Jamie felt more lighthearted than she had in days, and on the strength of an appointment made by one of the neighbor women to have her own portrait done, she turned into a tweed shop with thoughts of treating herself to a hand-woven skirt. Before she could enter, however, a familiar voice halted her, and wheeling about she discovered Avril at the curb, leaning from her Rolls-Royce.

As their glances met, Jamie recalled with a lurching heart Avril reading to her from Katrine's letter, and it was all she could do not to bolt and run.

But Avril called out cheerily, "Where are you off to, looking so jaunty?"

"I'm just doing a bit of shopping," Jamie answered, forcing a smile. "What about yourself?"

"I've finished mine and I'm going home for tea. Join me. It's a quarter past, but I'm sure Alex waited." Her lips turned up in a strange little smile. "I can't remember when I saw you last."

"At your house party, I believe," Jamie murmured. "Thanks very much for the invitation, but—"

Avril interrupted smoothly. "The house party. Of course. I promised to leave you alone afterward, didn't I? And see how well I've behaved? You can't refuse sharing tea with me."

Unwillingly, Jamie assented and in her Austin followed along behind the Rolls, thinking wryly that the two vehicles together must look like the tail end of a circus parade. Then as they turned into Avril's circular drive, Jamie's heart stopped. Parked before the entryway was the Ferrari.

Jamie's first thought was to run—to any place Ian wasn't. But before she could move, Avril was out of her own car. Poking her head through the window of the Austin, she said with mechanical brightness and just a shade of nervousness, "How delightful. Ian is here. However, I must warn you, Jamie. Don't mention Katrine."

Jamie stared back at her blankly. "Why not?"

"Ian is so impatient, so eager for the wedding to take place, that he goes into a regular rage whenever he hears Katrine's name." Avril's light laughter sounded strained, but her smile stayed bright. "He hates to be reminded that he must wait until her school year is over to claim her for his bride, and he simply can't bear the delay. The safer course is not to mention her at all."

Jamie nodded. She had witnessed one of Ian's rages, and she had no desire to see another. Actually, she dreaded seeing Ian in any mood, particularly in the presence of Avril and Alex, but she climbed glumly out of the car and followed Avril into the house.

Alex and Ian were having their tea on the terrace overlooking the loch. Pine trees overhead cast pleasant shadows and a soft breeze stirred the lilies bordering the flagstones.

Alex rose when he saw the ladies approaching, as did Ian, though rather tardily and with a bleak look at Jamie. She was grateful that Avril covered the embarrassing moment with a scolding remark.

"Naughty boys! You've started without us."

"I wouldn't have, darling"—Alex planted an affectionate kiss on his wife's cheek—"but Ian seems not to have eaten a thing in a week. I was afraid he might faint dead away if I didn't feed him at once. Ah, Jamie, my dear." He gave her a welcoming smile. "How are you? You've been avoiding us, I'm afraid."

"Not at all," Jamie murmured, taking the chair he offered beside him. "It's just that I've been very busy."

"With her painting." Avril set down her packages and slipped into a chair at Ian's side.

"Yes, I've just sold a portrait." Jamie spoke brightly, but she was scarcely aware of what she was saying. She had never seen Ian look so awful. There were dark shadows beneath his eyes and his face held a sad, dejected look. *Was he ill?*

"To whom, might I inquire?" said Alex.

For a moment Jamie couldn't think what he meant. "Oh—the portrait," she stammered finally. "To William MacPherson, the mechanic." She blushed then, and shot another swift look at Ian. "Actually, I used the portrait to pay a bill. But the occasion did result in one of their neighbor's wanting her own portrait painted." A nervous laugh escaped her. "So perhaps I've started a little business."

Ian eyed her with disapproval, but Alex, folding his hands over his portly front, said agreeably, "Oh, I should think so. If you can paint portraits, my dear, you'll have your hands full here. Everyone wants one—or six or a dozen. Look about our place." His sweeping gesture took in the mansion behind them. "The walls are covered with them, but there aren't any fine painters about anymore—only photographers. That's all we get." He shook his head in disgust. "Snap—and one comes away looking exactly as one does in a mirror."

"There's to be an art show in July," said Ian,

despite his disapproving stare. "In connection with the Highland Games at Inverness. Artists from all over the country will be showing their things there for sale."

"Perhaps I can exhibit there then." Jamie allowed herself a moment to look at him. He did appear ill. *The languishing bridegroom,* she thought bitterly.

Alex spoke up. "Yes, do look into it, Jamie. There's a fair held there along with the competitions —paintings, crafts, that sort of thing. The whole affair is an absolute delight. Plan to go down with Avril and me. Yes, you must be certain to." He bent to his teacup and finished in a murmur. "We're meeting the Grieves."

Jamie thought she saw a ghost of a smile flicker across Ian's drawn face, but it was gone before she was sure. Then Alex directed a muffled query to Ian. The sharp retort that followed startled them all.

"Blasted committee!" Ian burst out. His pale face darkened in a flush of anger. "I hope they drop off the edge of the earth before they contact me again."

Alex directed a look of concern at him. "Why, what do you mean, old boy?"

Avril cut in sharply. "Alex—! Please don't open an unpleasant subject."

"Is it unpleasant?" Her husband gave her a baffled look. "Ian has always been very much pro that Resettlement Group, hasn't he?" He looked to Ian for corroboration. "Haven't you, Ian?"

"I was, for as long as I thought they meant business," Ian retorted. "But now as far as I'm concerned they may all go to blazes."

Alex laughed uncomfortably. "Well, jolly good, if

they've offended you." Noticing Jamie's bewilderment, he turned to her with an explanation. "Perhaps you don't know, but the Resettlement Group, a committee of seven, was organized several years ago to work toward changing certain laws that would make it easier for Scotsmen in other parts of the world to come home and take up trusts and land grants that once belonged to their families but are now lying idle doing no good to anyone, least of all the country. Ian has worked very hard to make these changes come about."

"And pointless work it was," Ian growled. "First they sent me a wire demanding that I appear in Edinburgh for a crucial hearing, and after I break my neck getting there, what do I find but two members in the hospital and no progress made at all since the last time we met." Ian snorted in disgust. "I made the damned trip for nothing."

"Oh, surely not for nothing," said Alex. "I can't think you'd go to Edinburgh and not drop in on—"

Avril interrupted. "More tea, Ian?"

"No, thank you." He glanced irritably past her. "But it appears Jamie would oblige you. She's been holding her cup in midair for five minutes."

Color flooded Jamie's face. "None for me, thanks," she murmured. Blood roared in her ears. A committee had sent the telegram that had caused Ian to rush to Edinburgh? Not Katrine? She set the cup on its saucer and stood up. "It's time for me to go."

Swinging her gaze around to Avril, who was searching under her chair for a fallen napkin, she said evenly, "Will you see me to the door?"

"Why, yes, of course." Avril raised a flushed face.

"Stay where you are, Ian and Alex. I'll only be a minute."

In the cool hall Jamie turned to Avril with a challenging ring in her voice. "What happened to the letter?"

Avril arched her brows innocently. "What letter?"

"Katrine's letter to Ian. She didn't send it, did she?"

Avril offered an apologetic smile. "I'm afraid she didn't. She's such an impulsive girl. I should have known she might change her mind at the last minute. But then you saw what she wrote to me. Can you blame me for believing her? You were convinced, too, weren't you?" She took hold of Jamie's arm with icy fingers. "Didn't she sound like a girl madly in love?"

"Isn't she?" Jamie demanded. No wonder Ian had thought it none of her business to ask if he had seen Katrine! "Isn't she in love with him?"

"Of course she is. But half the time she doesn't know her own mind. One minute she's pouring her heart out in a letter to me, making grand plans—and the next she's fixed on her career again."

"Then what you told me as we were coming in about the wedding being postponed until the term is over—that wasn't true?"

"Perhaps it was a bit premature, but it will eventually be true," said Avril with a persuasive smile. "When Katrine is back in Applecross, seeing Ian each day—"

"But at present—" Jamie broke in. "As things

stand now, Ian and Katrine are no closer to marriage than they were when I came here, are they?"

Avril's eyes narrowed. She said unpleasantly, "What does your coming have to do with Ian's and Katrine's plans?"

"Nothing, of course." Jamie moistened her lips. "But I should know how things stand if I am to go on seeing Ian."

The icy hand on her arm tightened. "What do you mean, 'seeing' him?"

Jamie held steady, though her heart was pounding. "I meant that I'm sure to keep on running into him—as I did today, when you invited me to tea. I don't want to say anything that would upset him."

"Then don't mention his personal affairs," Avril said sharply. "However, because you and I are friends, I'll tell you this. Katrine is the only woman Ian has ever loved or ever will love. He adores her, but even if she doesn't marry him, he will never think seriously about anyone else."

She released Jamie's arm then and lifted the hand on which Alex's enormous diamond sparkled, turning it with undisguised satisfaction. "Ian's devotion to Katrine is complete—as Alex's is for me." She brought up her eyes and Jamie saw that it was her gaze that was icy now. "That's all you need to know, I think," she said crisply. "That ought to see you through any future conversations with Ian."

Chapter Nine

Driving home alone from Applecross, Jamie grew more irate with every mile. Obviously there was no limit to Avril's malice. Anyone listening to her there in the hall would have been able to see the lies churning out of her brain.

Naturally Katrine had not written to Ian, Jamie thought scornfully, *because she had not written to Avril, either!*

"Avril saw me kissing Ian," she said indignantly to the windshield, "and she raced right home and put her poisoned pen to the paper herself." And what havoc that forged letter had wreaked!

With an aching heart, Jamie recalled the miserable scene that had taken place at the croft when Ian returned from Edinburgh. Probably just as Ian had said, he had come to see if she was all right. But her defensive attitude, coupled with his, had led to a quarrel.

At the time, however, her hurt and anger were at least partially justified, she felt. With her own eyes she had seen what she believed was a declaration of love from Katrine. When Ian rushed off to Edinburgh, it had been natural for her to assume that he was responding to Katrine's personal declaration to him.

Now, of course, since she knew about the telegram from the Resettlement Committee, it was easy enough to see how stupidly she had behaved from Ian's viewpoint. Perhaps he had not even thought of Katrine. Jamie knew him well enough to know how all-consuming his interest in the crofters' way of life had become for him, and she could well imagine that the beastly mood he was in when he arrived at the cottage was due entirely to the letdown he felt after thinking that the moment was at hand when the situation might be resolved.

Oblivious to the glorious colors of the sunset fanning out ahead of her, Jamie tried as she drove to put herself in Ian's place. At Talbert Hall when she came down the stairs, he had been like a racehorse tethered at the starting post. He had wonderful news, and he had trusted her to understand that he hadn't time to share it with her, a trust based on their newfound intimacy of the afternoon.

All alone, Jamie felt her cheeks heat up. No wonder he had thought her sullen and selfish when she had turned her lips away and refused his kiss! The dark thoughts of Katrine that she was harboring, he had known nothing about.

And when he returned, she mused on—when he came to the croft, he had even told her that what had called him away had not turned out to be as significant as he had thought when he left her. But she had been too intent on nourishing her anger to listen. She had not, in fact, until this moment recalled those words at all, but only his biting remark that her thoughts were always on herself.

Sick at heart, Jamie turned into the croft lane, regretting for once that her little cottage was so isolated. The long evening ahead with only her miserable self for company loomed as a dreadful prospect.

But by the time she had changed into a pair of faded jeans and the soft blue shirt she often wore when she painted, she had cheered herself up a bit. The important thing to remember, she told herself as she sat at her little table over a bite of supper, was that a misunderstanding was the principal wedge between herself and Ian—that, and the bitter words that had followed.

Even if—as Alex seemed about to suggest—Ian had dropped in on Katrine, it would appear from the look of him that the meeting had not gone well. It seemed safe to assume that Katrine was no closer to accepting Ian's proposal than she had ever been—even Avril admitted that—and if such were the case, then there was still a chance—however slight—that Ian might once again turn to her.

That was humbling herself, Jamie thought uneasily. *That was truly taking crumbs from Katrine's table.* But at this point pride seemed unimportant. It was pride that had spoiled things with Ian before. To let it come between them again would be monstrous.

Shoving back from the table, she stood up with fresh resolution. She must speak with Ian tonight. And this time it was she who must go to him.

Talbert Hall was ablaze with light when Jamie turned the Austin into the long driveway that led to the mansion. Despite the resolve that had propelled her thus far, she hesitated when she saw that even the large drawing room was lit.

Was Ian entertaining guests?

She looked askance at the faded denims she had not taken time to change and at the soft blue shirt streaked with paint. Once before he had accused her of dressing like a peat-cutter. What would he say now, particularly if she were nervy enough to barge into the midst of his company?

Wracked by indecision, she sat for a few minutes in the Austin with the engine and the lights shut off, staring at the castle. Some of the heavy draperies were drawn back, but she could see only an occasional figure moving through the rooms, so apparently there wasn't a party in progress. No cars were parked in the driveway, either, not even the Ferrari. Disappointment gripped her. *Perhaps Ian wasn't there. Perhaps the servants were responsible for all the lights, busy with some special project in the master's absence.*

For another minute she hesitated, and then with a grim set to her lips threw open the door of the car and started up the walk. She had come this far, she told herself staunchly. She would never forgive herself if she lacked the courage at the last minute to at least see if Ian were at home or not.

Pressing the bell with firm fingers, she waited, but when after a moment the heavy door swung back, she felt her legs turn to jelly. Ian himself stood glowering before her.

"I expected Robert to answer," she murmured, naming the butler.

Ian covered his own surprise at finding Jamie on

his doorstep with a curt query. "Was it Robert you came to see?"

"I came to see you." Jamie lifted her chin defiantly. "But if you're busy—"

"I am." He scowled down at her. "So is Robert and so are the upstairs maids and the downstairs footmen and even the cook's boy. But I suppose one more joining the search will make no difference." He stepped aside and impatiently waved her in.

Torn between anger at his rudeness and her resolve to straighten things out between them at any cost, Jamie moved into the entryway. "May I ask what you're looking for?"

"An inventory," said Ian.

Beyond him in the small drawing room, Jamie could see Robert emptying out a drawer from a Victorian desk, and bent over the contents of the piano bench was the little maid who had served Jamie during her stay at the Hall.

Jamie turned back toward the door. "Everyone seems terribly busy—"

"By heaven, they'd better be," said Ian grimly.

"I'll come another time."

But Ian caught hold of her arm. "As long as you're here, you may as well make yourself useful," he said gruffly. "Come along. You can start in the study."

The study, Jamie discovered, had already been thoroughly ransacked. Every drawer of the desk was turned out; its top looked as if a cyclone had recently blown through. And in the wall beside the fireplace a safe she had not even known was there stood open, spilling its valuables onto the rug.

"What a bloody business!" said Ian, sweeping up a handful of papers from the carpet. "I can see the damned thing as plain as day, but where in heaven's name is it?"

Jamie's innate sense of order shoved all other considerations into the background. "Sit down," she commanded. "There in your chair. Sit perfectly still and tell me, please, as calmly as you can, just what sort of inventory it is that's lost and where you saw it last and what it looks like."

With a frank look of relief, Ian did as he was told. "Thank God somebody else is capable of giving a few orders. I've been barking out commands for over an hour, and what have I turned up? Not a damned thing."

Seeing the ordinarily controlled Ian as harried as any housewife who has mislaid her account book amused Jamie, but she held back her smile. "Apparently, what you've lost is something quite important."

"It's needed for a tax report." Ian sighed explosively. "I must have it tomorrow, and if I don't have it there'll be all kinds of snags and snarls to get through until I can produce a duplicate. I could be tied up for months."

"A duplicate of what?" said Jamie patiently.

"It goes back to when the Hall was redecorated. I made up my mind to get rid of eight or ten marble pieces that had been in the family for ages: buxom ladies eating grapes; wall-eyed senators orating—that sort of thing. Depressing objects I've never liked. Finally, Avril found an overseas buyer and got a fat price for them that I promptly reinvested in property improvements. Now I've got to turn up with the inventory of the sale to settle up the taxes, and I haven't got the blasted thing."

"What you've lost is the only record of the sale?"

"No, thank heaven, but it was the only one signed by the buyer. The man travels constantly, and Avril spent a miserable few weeks trying to track him down. Finally, Katrine located him through a friend of hers and got the signature. Who knows where he is now, or if we'll ever find him again?"

"Have you contacted Avril? She may remember where you put it. She may even have it herself."

Ian sighed again. "She doesn't. I remember when she gave it to me. It was the morning of the day you arrived, as a matter of fact. I was in Applecross checking on another matter, and she sent Alex out to the Jeep with it. A large sheet of pink paper. I can see it now with the sleet spattering on it."

"Pink paper?" Jamie tensed. "A list on pink paper?"

"Yes, that's right. A wretched shade, more raspberry than pink, actually."

"Oh, Ian." With a fearful look at him, Jamie wilted into a chair, but he seemed not to notice how swiftly her air of authority had vanished.

"We've turned the place upside down," he went on in the same dismal tone. "I've even had Robert checking in the wine cellar. It isn't here. It simply isn't here."

Jamie took a long breath. "Maybe that's because I have it."

Ian's head shot up. "What?"

"I think I have your inventory—or I did have it." Jamie's violet eyes looked twice their size in her pale face. "Are you terribly angry? I didn't know it was important."

Ian leaned across the desk, his face creased with astonishment. "What are you saying?"

"Don't you remember? The evening you looked at my sketches I mentioned the list. I found it in the Jeep the day you were in the tobacconist's when I needed paper quickly to sketch the mechanic's boy with his strawberries."

"My Lord—" Ian came out of his chair. "You haven't thrown it away, have you?"

Her voice trembled as she rose. "I don't know. I don't think so. Oh, Ian, surely I haven't!"

Within five minutes after they reached the cottage, Jamie had located the inventory amid her stacks of sketches and handed it over to Ian.

"Does it matter that it's been drawn upon?" she said anxiously as Ian tucked it away in the pocket of his jacket.

"Not to me." He seemed to have shed ten years when Jamie produced the list. "And I couldn't care less what the tax fellow thinks. He'll have his signature. That's all he's after."

"I'm dreadfully sorry to have caused such a bother."

"It's more my fault than yours," said Ian generously. "But the thing is, as I told you, I remember being rather careful with it." His dark brows drew together in a frown. "I distinctly remember laying it in the back seat with two other documents which turned up this evening exactly where I thought they would. What I can't understand is why the inventory wasn't with them."

"I think I know." Jamie sat down at the table, inviting Ian with her eyes to do the same. "It came to me as we were driving over." She bit her lip. "Oh, this is my fault, too, I'm afraid. Honestly, I shouldn't blame you if you never speak to me again."

Ian surprised her by reaching across and taking her hand in his. "Stop heaping coals on your head," he chided gently. "All's well that ends well. However, if you have a theory, I want to hear it."

The warmth of his skin on hers set Jamie's blood racing, but she kept her voice steady. "The day you rescued me on the road you had the back seat of the Jeep crammed with my luggage. Do you recall that? And then when you turned off to look for the lamb, everything came tumbling onto the floor; my paints scattered—"

Ian chuckled. "I'm not likely to forget that."

"That's when it happened, I'm sure," said Jamie. "Your pink paper slid under the seat and didn't show up again until I was scrambling around looking for something to draw on."

Ian let go of her hand, but his eyes went on examining her with disturbing slowness. "You're a regular Sherlock Holmes, aren't you, Miss MacPherson."

Her heart lurched at the familiar rolling sound of the "r" as he said her name. *His name, too . . . theirs.* She dropped her gaze to hide her look of love. "Anyway, I'm glad we found it," she murmured.

"But there's one mystery still unsolved." He paused, waiting until she looked at him again. "Why did you come to the Hall tonight?"

Color flooded her face. "I'm afraid I had another apology to make."

A smile lifted the corners of his tantalizing lips. "This is certainly your evening, isn't it?"

The carefully worded explanation she had contrived on the way to the Hall had long ago forsaken her. What could she say now, she wondered, that would make him understand how she really felt and yet not leave her completely vulnerable?

He broke the silence, eyes twinkling. "Out with it. What other sins have you committed?"

The chief one was falling in love with you. The confession sprang to her lips, but she held it back. "I wanted to apologize for my rudeness when you came here to the cottage after your return from Edinburgh."

The stiff little statement seemed to amuse him. "As I recall," he said with another smile, "I behaved rather unpleasantly myself."

"But only because I did," she blurted out quickly. "Until today I didn't understand about the telegram."

"Oh. I see." His look darkened.

"But this afternoon, when you were describing to Alex what happened—"

He broke in. "Why did you need it spelled out for you? Why couldn't you have trusted me at the time without getting angry?"

"I wasn't angry."

"Oh, weren't you? You were boiling mad. You turned your face away from me."

"But not because I didn't want to kiss you."

"Then why didn't you?"

"Because— Oh, I can't explain. Won't you trust *me* now? There was a misunderstanding. It's all so complicated."

"On the contrary. I think it's quite simple. You resented the fact that something more important than yourself required my immediate attention."

Jamie's temper flared. "If I'd been as secretive as you, wouldn't you have resented it?"

A muscle twitched in his jaw. "I hope I would have had enough faith in you to respect your decision."

"Then respect it now, Ian! I have decided not to tell you why I felt resentful, because I think it's best not to. Can't we let it go at that?"

His gaze hardened. "I was not the one who introduced this subject."

"Oh, Ian!" Flinging pride to the winds, she reached across the table and took his hands in hers. "A few minutes ago we were happy together. Why must we always quarrel?"

For a long moment he looked at her. Then suddenly the tightness around his mouth relaxed and he brought her fingertips to his lips. "What a firebrand you are," he muttered huskily. "But with all that, I admire your spirit."

Jamie was trembling. "Do you?"

"I think you know I do."

His hoarse answer sent shivers up her spine. The look he had fixed on her was a look of love. She was certain that it was!

"Ian—" Her voice came out a whisper. "Pretend with me that we've only now returned from Eilean Maree. That we never quarreled. That you never went to Edinburgh."

They came up from the table together and into each other's arms. Ian brought her swiftly to his chest and held her fast, his lean lines hardening against her body. His lips parted hers in a kiss, deep and mesmerizing. The blood in Jamie's veins turned to a heady wine, bubbling, dancing. "Ian—oh, Ian!"

He held her closer, the buttons of his jacket cutting into her breast. She felt the pressure of his thighs, one hand moving in the small of her back, the other at the nape of her neck, his fingers smoothing her flesh, tangling in her hair.

"Jamie—" His hot breath curled in her ear. "The time we've wasted. The agony we might have spared ourselves—" Then they were lost again in a storm of passion, swaying together in a sensual, erotic rhythm that stirred them both to the brink of surrender.

Finally, they came away from each other, shaken and breathless. Almost at once Ian reached for her again, but with lips throbbing from his kiss, she begged him: "Come, sit down."

Following her, he took the chair that faced hers, his heavy-lidded gaze sweeping over her, drawing her to him, but she held onto the arms of her own chair until the wild pulsing of her body gradually subsided. When she could speak calmly again, she said, "You frightened me this afternoon. You looked so weary, so ill. Have you been that worried about this tax matter?"

"Not that—" he said huskily. "Until I got home from Applecross, I didn't even know the inventory was missing." He fixed a smoldering gaze on her parted lips. "It's you I've worried about. It seems a year since we quarreled, but when I saw you at Alex's I got angry all over again at how obstinate you were, how aloof."

"That isn't how I felt! I missed you terribly. Oh, Ian—what if tonight hadn't happened?"

Pinpoints of light glowed hotly in his eyes.

"It had to happen. We had to find each other again. Now nothing can keep us apart."

But so much already had. Could it again? A shiver of apprehension rippled over Jamie. "Ian—" She passed her tongue over her lips, buying time as she watched him. "What about Katrine?"

His answer came quickly, carelessly. "What about her?"

"You cared very much for her."

A flicker of annoyance appeared in his eyes. "I've told you, that's over."

"Is it? Is it, Ian?"

He set his jaw stubbornly. "Katrine and I are friends—that's all. Do you understand?"

A chill took hold of Jamie. She wished she could be certain of that, but how soon would it be before doubt assailed her again, as it had done when Ian had rushed off to Edinburgh?

Fighting off the desolate feeling that thought inspired, she got to her feet. "I'll make a pot of tea."

"None for me," Ian said. He stood—angrily, she thought. But when she passed his chair, he caught her wrist and pulled her to him, his hot gaze sliding over her. "No more questions, Jamie," he muttered hoarsely. "Katrine is in the past. It's you, my darling, who belongs to the future."

A dizzying surge of love welled up inside her. Reason deserted her, and she closed her eyes and brought her lips to his. Swiftly he took them, his own moving feverishly upon her mouth, his arms enfolding her so that her body molded against his and she felt the full force of his ardor in the hardened muscles that swelled against her flesh. Near the hearth a cricket began a song, but Jamie heard nothing except the roar of blood against her eardrums and the sweet muffled sounds of love spilling from Ian's tongue. Their passion heightened, lifting them to a new plane of arousal.

Then from a distance Jamie heard her own voice, annoyingly practical. "Ian— We've forgotten Robert and the others. We should have told them we thought we'd found the paper."

Ian cursed softly and drew back. "Lord—they're probably sifting the flour by now. I'd better go."

She clung to him, murmuring. "Maybe it's lost again. Maybe you don't even have it now."

He took her arms down from his neck and brought the paper out of his pocket. He made a great thing of unfolding it and then said solemnly, "Why, you're right. This is only a grocery list."

Jamie snatched it from him, half-afraid to laugh, and for the first time she brought her full attention to bear on it. " 'Two Ionian marbles, blue-veined—' " She stopped reading suddenly. The letters, bold and black, leaped up at her from the page.

"Ian—" Her mouth tightened. "Who did you say got this signature? Katrine?"

He nodded.

"But Avril wrote out the list, of course."

Half-annoyed at her persistence, he shook his head. "Katrine wrote it. She took it down over the telephone."

"She couldn't have," Jamie insisted, feeling a

desperate enough need to set straight the matter of
the lie. "I saw a letter from her once. I know her
writing."

With a sigh, Ian took the paper from her. "You
have a fixation about Katrine, do you realize that?"

Then his look softened and he pulled her into his
arms again. "I'll tell you something. Avril writes like
a languishing maiden out of the eighteenth century,
all wispy and wobbly. But not Katrine. Katrine
makes her letters with the same determination with
which she pursues everything else." He held up the
paper again, smiling grimly. "Look at them—they're
like soldiers marching into battle."

Chapter Ten

Jamie was still pondering the problem of Katrine's handwriting long after Ian had strolled off whistling across the moor, leaving behind the promise that he would return in the morning with plans for them to spend the day together.

His insistence that Katrine had written the inventory had not wavered, and Jamie was certain that the handwriting was the same as that on the letter Avril had shown her—the letter that only that afternoon she had been so certain had been written by Avril herself. The same bold, heavy strokes. As Ian had said—like soldiers marching into battle. An apt description that chilled her.

Convinced that Avril had written the letter, Jamie had been able to let the threat of Katrine's interest in Ian recede again into the indefinite past as she had done the day they went to the Gairloch Peninsula. But if the letter Avril had shown her had actually come from Katrine, as obviously it had, then once again Katrine posed a threat.

Still, she tried to comfort herself, *Katrine had not followed through*. It was not her letter, but the telegram from the Resettlement Committee that had drawn Ian to Edinburgh. Unless— Her blood congealed. *Unless Ian had lied.*

The torture of doubt haunted her through most of the night. Toward morning she drifted into a troubled sleep, but after a few hours she woke up with the same uncertainties. Finally, she dragged herself out of bed and at nine was sitting by the cold hearth with a cup of tea when Ian appeared at the door.

Not a trace of yesterday's fatigue appeared on his face, and in his hand he held a bouquet, picked that morning from the Talbert Hall garden and still sparkling with dew.

"Pocketbook plant," he said authoritatively, pointing out stems of cunning, golden blooms spotted with red. "Shasta daisies, campanula, phlox and candy lilies," he finished with a flourish, pressing the flowers into her arms and then bending to place a good-morning kiss on her lips.

"They're beautiful," Jamie breathed, burying her face in the blossoms for their fragrance, but partly, too, out of embarrassment that Ian had caught her not yet dressed. But the sight of him on her doorstep had lifted her spirits, and as she brought down Uncle Angus's pewter pitcher from the cupboard shelf and plunged the flower stems into the water, she asked herself what her long night of worry had been about.

Even if Ian had made up the business about the Resettlement Committee meeting to hide from her the fact that he wanted to see Katrine, he was here now, not in Edinburgh. He wanted to be with her, not Katrine, and every moment they were together she wanted him to remember as pure joy.

"What shall I wear?" she called out from the bedroom. "Where are we going?"

"We're going to Kinshiel," Ian replied, "to a sheep auction."

Through the closed door Jamie laughed. "A sheep auction!" *How romantic!* "What is the appropriate form of dress for that?"

"The same as for a woolen mill, I imagine," he answered. "And since that's where we're headed afterward, wear whatever you like."

Jamie chose a plaid skirt and a soft mauve blouse that brought out the deeper hues of her violet eyes and made her porcelain skin appear even more delicate. When she emerged from the bedroom, Ian's gaze moved over her with obvious approval. "I'm glad you wore comfortable shoes," he said, but his eyes were on the clinging blouse that molded her breasts, and he drew her to him for a deep, tender kiss that left her longing for another when he let her go. While she was dressing, the troubled thoughts that had made her night miserable had lifted like a moorland mist, and now she felt as refreshed and eager for the day as if the sun itself had risen inside her.

Seeing her sparkle, Ian bestowed another swift kiss and then led her off to the waiting Ferrari.

Kinshiel was a comfortable-looking little town tucked away in a glen not many miles from Applecross. The houses, of gray stone with sturdy slate roofs, were perched along a murmuring river whose waters were clear as crystal. In every dooryard bright red geraniums bloomed. Stone porches stood wet from scrubbing and lace-curtained windows sparkled in the sunlight.

The sheep auction was well under way when they

arrived, and though Jamie was a bit uncomfortable when she saw she was the only woman in attendance, the kilted buyers who sat hunched on wooden platforms surrounding the ring welcomed her with warm smiles, pulling in their rubber-booted feet as she and Ian passed along in front of them, searching for seats. Soon Ian was engaged with the other men in the subtle signals that indicated their bids, and while Jamie watched, fascinated, more money exchanged hands than she had seen in the whole of her lifetime.

Ian was exhilarated afterward, being particularly pleased that a flock of white-faced Cheviots, for which he and a tall farmer in a MacNichol tartan had bid spiritedly, had fallen into his possession. The woolen mill was only a few blocks away, and as they walked along, he spoke animatedly of the superior qualities of Cheviot wool, which made it the best for dying.

"The fibers hold their brilliance," he explained, and as he showed her through the mill, she saw firsthand the blending of the blues and blacks with the undyed wool. The combination then was spun into variegated yarn. Listening to Ian's knowledgeable comments as they moved along, Jamie wondered that a man of Ian's experience and ability in such a wide range of activities could find her interesting.

All her doubts, however, were swept away when, late in the afternoon, Ian parked the Jeep in the glen where Kinshiel's bubbling river cut through a marsh.

With his arms holding her close, she felt truly certain for the first time that he loved her. Never had she felt more in tune with another person, never more adored.

The day had been perfect, but Ian had scarcely touched her since they left the cottage. Now his warm endearments, his sensuous lips on her throat and eyelids, his strong, caressing hands smoothing her skin told her in a language of their own how much he cared for her. She longed with all her heart to hear the actual words *I love you,* but that would come in time, she prayed, snuggling against his chest. For now just his nearness was enough.

"Do you know what I keep remembering?" he said after a while.

"Tell me," said Jamie, reveling in the virile scent of his sun-warmed skin.

With erotic slowness Ian traced the angle of her cheekbone. "I keep seeing you," he teased, "that day you were standing so haughtily out there in the sleet beside your stranded Austin."

Jamie sat up. "How awful of you to remember that!" she said indignantly.

"You were like some deposed queen." Ian's throaty chuckle brought reluctant laughter from Jamie, too.

He said, "I was so angry at you for having me drive you all the way to Applecross and then accusing me of being a sheepherder impersonating myself."

"You looked like a sheepherder!"

"I had such fine plans that day for Jamie MacPherson."

She smiled impishly. "And I spoiled them all."

"Never mind. I laid new ones." His crooked grin

made her heart turn over. Bringing her to him, he muttered huskily, "I have a surprise for you."

Pulling from his pocket a small black box, he snapped the lid up. Inside, set high in a ring of brushed gold, a translucent gemstone sparkled with amber radiance.

Jamie caught her breath. "Ian!"

He said quickly, "Of course it's not an engagement ring." Intent on slipping it onto a finger of her right hand, he missed the swift flush that darkened her cheeks. "But it's something rather special, anyway."

He lifted his gaze, and she prayed he would not see the disappointment she was sure showed plainly in her eyes.

"It's a *cairngorm,*" he said. "A topaz quartz. Not so valuable and not so enduring as a diamond, but a pure, native stone. A true stone. And unblemished."

He took her face in his hands as if it were a flower and kissed her mouth gently. "You're a *cairngorm,* Jamie. And with your sparkle, you've brought light into my life."

The weeks flew by. Jamie had never known such happiness. Each morning when she woke up in her little cottage, her thoughts flew first to Ian and then to the ring on her finger. Oh, the promise that little circle of gold symbolized!

And yet, one cloud remained on the horizon. Ian had still not confessed his love for her. He behaved like a man in love. He spent every evening with her, but always he stopped short of that final declaration she was yearning so to hear.

Katrine had not been mentioned again, and whole days passed when Jamie did not even think of her. But she had not had Avril to remind her, either. She and Alex were entertaining English friends, Ian had told her, and they had been away a great deal of the time seeing the sights.

The same evening that he mentioned the Stuarts, he mentioned something else that for a moment, at least, had almost made Jamie's heart stop.

"Perhaps I should tell you that *cairngorms,*" he said casually as he held her in his arms, "in these parts, at any rate, are often given as bethrothal stones."

But almost as quickly, he shattered her hopes. "A silly custom," he went on, "but I saw no reason to let it prevent me from giving you the ring of my choice." He passed his lips over her cheek. "But if you want to avoid calling forth a lot of raised eyebrows and embarrassing questions, perhaps you'll want to leave off the ring whenever you go into Applecross."

Jamie swallowed. "I don't mind embarrassing questions."

"Suit yourself, then," he said with a shrug.

For an instant she was too hurt to register the full import of his meaning. Then like a brick it hit her. He wanted to keep secret the fact that he cared for her! Or perhaps this meant that he really did not care—that he was only amusing himself with her until Katrine returned from Edinburgh.

A surge of shame and anger spawned a heated reply. "I intend to show the ring to one person in Applecross," she challenged. "Or else I shan't keep it."

Turning her in his arms, he gazed quizzically down at her. "Who is that?"

"Avril."

He frowned. "Why Avril, in heaven's name?"

"Because—" She was almost too terrified to speak. Was she cutting off her nose to spite her face? But she went on, taking a deep breath. "I think it only fair that Avril be made aware of what good friends we have become. She makes no secret of the fact that she considers you Katrine's property, so I can't go on seeing you in this . . ."—she ran her tongue across her lips— ". . . in this new way without letting her know that I am."

Ian looked at her for a moment, and then the corners of his mouth turned up in tolerant amusement. "What a righteous little person you are," he murmured. But he said it tenderly and followed it at once with a kiss that made her forget how deeply he had hurt her.

Later, though, she mulled over the conversation again, convincing herself at last that Ian had meant exactly what he said and nothing more. People in Applecross might misunderstand, might think they were "engaged to be engaged." He was only warning her. *If she didn't mind,* his shrug had said, *then neither did he.* And he had made no final objection to her speaking to Avril, either, so gradually she was able to relax.

But she did not forget the matter.

On the Saturday before the Highland Games, Jamie decided to go into Applecross. Long ago she had finished the portrait of William MacPherson's neighbor, Sara Campbell, but busy in her new joy, she had put off delivering it.

Using that as a pretext, she avoided telling Ian that she also planned to see Avril. In her moments of soul-searching, she had been forced to admit that part of her reason for wanting to show Avril the ring was pure pride. She wanted Avril to know that here was proof positive of Ian's affection—not exactly the motive of the "righteous little person" Ian had accused her of being—but human, certainly!

However, when she reached the Stuart mansion, she sensed at once that Alex and Avril were still away. The place had a desolate closed look. She had read in the local newspaper that their friends had returned to England. Perhaps Avril and Alex had accompanied them, she thought, and was surprised at how disappointed she felt. She rang the bell and received no response, but in a moment a gardener appeared from around the terrace. When he recognized Jamie, he called out, "Everyone has gone to Inverness, Miss. It's the games, you know."

Nodding, Jamie thanked him, then turned away in dismay. She had given over the morning to working up the courage to face Avril, and she felt deflated at not being able to bring the matter to a conclusion.

Of course, she had nothing to be ashamed of, she reminded herself as she drove along on her way to Sara Campbell's. But still her conscience nagged her a bit. She had judged Avril unfairly once, and she hated now to feel she had betrayed her, too, by listening to her confidences concerning Katrine and at the same time falling in love with Ian. Not that it had happened as purposefully as that, but there was little chance that Avril would see the matter any other way. Naturally, this would put an end to their friendship. She wouldn't grieve over that because she had never really cared for Avril, but it worried her that Ian's and Alex's longstanding regard for each other might suffer through this fault of hers.

She was still regretting that the confrontation she had dreaded for days had not come to pass when she arrived at Sara Campbell's neat white cottage. For the next hour and a half she and Sara lugged the portrait through the rooms, trying it first on one wall and then on another. At last they settled on the first space they tried—above the mantel. Then nothing would do but that Jamie stay on for tea while friends were called in to admire Sara's new acquisition and to congratulate the artist.

As Jamie expected, when she arrived back at the croft, Ian was waiting for her. He had parked the Ferrari near the door and was leaning against the fender gazing at the sunset with his arms folded across his chest in the manner of a patient martyr.

"I was on the verge of sending out a search party," he called as she got out of the Austin. "What in heaven's name took you so long?"

"You aren't cross, are you, darling?" Smiling, Jamie lifted her face for his kiss. "I'm sorry to be late, but—"

"But you went to Avril's," he finished for her, a wry grin replacing his frown. "Well, what did Lady Stuart say? I suppose she chewed you out for horning in on Katrine's territory."

Jamie flushed. So he had known all along what her real reason had been for going! "Avril wasn't at home, Mr. Know-It-All. And what makes you so sure I went there, anyway?"

"My darling—" He trailed kisses across her cheek

as they strolled toward the cottage. "I know you like a book. Besides"—he cut his eyes toward the ring on her finger—"you wore the *cairngorm* to back up your claim." He shook his head in mock despair. "Avril may have missed your announcement, but by now everyone else in Applecross knows. I should have warned you. Sara Campbell is a much more faithful dispenser of news than the weekly paper."

"Sara Campbell didn't see my ring," said Jamie archly. "I put it in my purse before I went into her house."

Ian stopped before the door and pulled her against him, touching her brow with his lips and then planting a lingering kiss on her mouth. When he let her go, he murmured, "Where were Avril and Alex?"

"Already gone to Inverness." Jamie led the way into the house, welcoming the glad sense of home she always felt when she entered it. Turning to Ian, she smoothed his broad shoulders with a loving possessiveness and bestowed a kiss of her own.

"Do you know," she said with a daring she had not thought herself capable of, "the first time I crossed this threshold, you carried me."

He laughed, and she felt the sound ripple over her like a caress. "What a romantic you are."

She tipped her head back for a straight look at him. "Do you object to my being romantic?"

"I don't object to anything about you, my darling idiot—except that you're too busy with things that don't include me. Do you realize that every day this week you've been off to Loch Carron painting heaven-knows-what, while I've been cooling my heels at the hall?"

"I've saved every evening for you!" she protested. "Besides, you've been busy with things of your own."

"Things I've invented because you had no time for me," he complained, only half in jest.

Jamie's eyes opened wide. "You're jealous! Jealous of paint and brushes and canvas. Shame on you!" But secretly she was delighted. Ian missed being with her as much as she missed him.

"Why do you have to spend so much time at it?" he grumbled.

"Because it's an art, and art requires hours and hours of practice."

Ian's gaze went to one side of the room, where Jamie's canvases were stacked against the wall. "If you stop now," he said, "we'll have just enough scenes of Loch Carron at sunset to fill every blank space in Talbert Hall."

Jamie laughed, but her violet eyes lost their sparkle. "You're serious, aren't you? You'd like me to give up painting." *He had wanted Katrine to give up medicine, too.*

"Not give it up altogether." He moved away toward the chairs in the sitting room. "But I'd like to know that you've saved some time for me in your life."

"But of course I have!" She came to him quickly. "All the most important hours. These canvases, and my preoccupation with them—it's all because of the Inverness exhibit. I want to have enough work to make a creditable display. And to make a little money, too," she added with an anxious look.

"Oh, please try to understand." Her eyes entreated him. "All my life I've felt a need to prove that I could paint, and that I could support myself doing it. For my own satisfaction I have to do this, Ian. I need this one opportunity to prove to myself what I'm capable of." She paused, the light from the lamp gilding the fine planes of her face. "Won't you give me your support?"

With a muffled groan he pulled her to him. "Can I deny you anything?"

They kissed. *It's all right,* Jamie exulted. *He doesn't really mind.* But at the back of her mind a tiny residue of uneasiness would not be entirely dismissed.

During the simple supper that she fixed for them, however, her anxiety dimmed, and when they were clearing away the dishes, she felt enough confidence in his approval to ask another favor.

"Will you drive me to Inverness, Ian?"

"Minx," he said roughly, pretending annoyance. "Give you an inch and you take a mile. You're shameless."

She laughed. "Only because I'm desperate. Alex invited me to go with them, and now I've found out he's left without me." A sudden thought struck her, and she turned to Ian with narrowed eyes. "Did you by any chance have anything to do with that?"

Ian gazed at the ceiling. "Perhaps I did mention to Alex that day at tea that if you went, I'd be taking you."

Jamie glowered playfully. "Just for that, I'll go alone in my Austin."

"You won't if you want to get there," Ian answered complacently. "MacPherson is a fine mechanic, but even he can't turn a pumpkin into a chariot. A few more hills, and your fine automobile is likely to be ready for the scrap heap."

When the kitchen was tidy again, they set out for a stroll down the lane. Darkness came later each evening, and Jamie was glad as they moved along with fingers entwined that enough was left of the day's light for them to enjoy together.

This was home, she thought with a surge of longing. If only Ian would love her enough to let her stay with him forever. From the warmth of his hand she drew a tingling sense of arousal. Did she dare dream that one day they would be married? That she would never need to be without the solid shelter of his love?

Ian broke into her thoughts with a question. "Were you disappointed this afternoon when you missed Avril?"

"A little." Jamie felt again the pang of guilt that had assailed her earlier. "But it doesn't matter. I'll have plenty of opportunities to see her in Inverness, I imagine." She smiled up at him. "Why do you suppose she and Alex left for the games so early? They don't start until Monday, do they?"

"No, they began in the middle of the week. It's the exhibitions that start on Monday. Actually, though, I suspect they went before time because, according to Alex, they're house partying with the Grieves."

"Oh, dear." Jamie rolled her eyes. "I lucked out there, didn't I?"

"You call it luck?" Ian chided. "It was I who saved you, my lass."

She gave him a quick kiss. "Then I'm eternally grateful."

"Never mind," he answered. "I owe you one. You

saved me from a fate far worse than the Grieves when you turned up with my inventory." He drew her arm into the crook of his elbow and smoothed her slender fingertips. "By the way, what did you mean that night when you said you'd once seen a letter from Katrine. Where? Whose was it?"

"Oh—" The letter! After all this time! Jamie wondered if Ian could hear the pounding of her heart. "It was Avril's. She showed it to me," she said faintly.

"Why?" Ian halted in the soft turf of the lane and turned to look at her. Above his shoulder a thin rind of moon hung in a sky falsely blue and a pale star blinked beside it.

Jamie swallowed. She had already deceived Ian once today and hated herself for having done so. It had been a pointless deception, and she had no wish to go on hiding things from him. Besides, if she were to have any hopes for the future, then sooner or later she must know for certain whether or not Katrine had any power over their lives. Why not tell him the truth?

Still she hesitated while her heart pumped furiously. "Are you sure you want to know?"

Ian's abrupt laughter rang out in the still air. "Is it some terrible dark secret?"

"In a way, yes."

"Then, by all means, tell me. I'd wager Sara Campbell knows. Why shouldn't I?"

Jamie took a long breath. "Katrine wrote to Avril—" Her lungs emptied. "And told her that she had changed her mind, that she had decided to marry you, after all."

Ian stared down at her. "What? What are you saying?"

"It was ages ago, Ian!" Jamie said quickly. "At the house party. The evening you and I planned to leave and didn't. Avril came to my room at bedtime with the letter. She insisted I read it, but I wouldn't, and so she read it to me. . . ."

Ian's incredulous stare unnerved Jamie. She ran the tip of her tongue across her lips. She wasn't sure how she had expected him to react, but certainly not with that stunned, blank look. Had she misjudged his feelings entirely? Panic seized her. Did Katrine mean so much to him, after all?

Words spilled pell-mell from her lips. "Katrine wasn't sincere, Ian. She said that she was writing the same thing to you, that she was sending your letter out in the same post. But she didn't. It would have been waiting for you at the Hall if she had, and there was only that telegram from the committee." Ian's strained stillness made Jamie's throat close, and she struggled for breath to finish. "I didn't know that, though. I thought it *was* her letter. I thought that was why you dropped everything and rushed to Edinburgh. That was what I resented and could never explain. Do you understand?"

"Yes." He seemed to look straight through her. "I think at last I'm beginning to."

"But it doesn't matter now." She clutched his arm. "Does it, Ian?"

He focused on her suddenly. "Certainly it matters," he said harshly. "How could you possibly think it wouldn't?" He took hold of her shoulders in an iron grip. "Start over," he commanded. "Tell me everything that happened. Tell me exactly what was in the letter."

In a trembling voice and sick with dread, Jamie made her recital. Anguished, she searched Ian's face for some sign of reassurance, but the look he fixed on her was a stranger's—hard and uncompromising and totally incomprehensible.

"You've known this for weeks," he said when she finished. "Why didn't you tell me?"

"Why should I have?" Jamie's mouth was powder-dry. "Nothing came of it."

"That's beside the point. Can't you see that?" Jamie flinched as his powerful fingers bit into her flesh. "We quarreled. We were angry at each other. We might never have been reconciled—"

Never, thought Jamie, *except for me!* The earth tilted crazily. "You're hurting me—"

But before the words were out, Ian abruptly released her. "I have to see Katrine." In long strides he started up the lane toward the Ferrari.

Jamie came after him, her black hair flying, her face stark in the dim light of the fading day. "You're going to her? You're going to Katrine?"

"I have to." He flung the words over his shoulder. Reaching the car, he got inside and slammed the door.

Jamie stood on the other side of it, her throat so tight with pain she could scarcely speak. "If you leave now and go to Edinburgh, I won't be here when you get back."

"I understand that. I'm sorry." The roar of the motor all but drowned out his words, tossed distract-edly through the window as he put the car in gear.

"The best I can offer you is the Jeep. Take it. Don't go out on the road in the Austin."

Jamie gasped. He was making absolutely certain she was gone when he returned with Katrine. Tears spilled over onto her cheeks. "I wouldn't take your Jeep if you tied it up in ribbons!"

"Wait a minute—" Ian leaned out of the window. "There's no need for *you* to be upset." But Jamie was gone. The cottage door slammed. For a moment the Ferrari lingered in the lane, its motor throbbing. Then in a sudden spurt of energy, it shot off across the moor.

Chapter Eleven

Jamie had passed through Inverness before on her way to Applecross in March. Then she had appreciated the quaint Victorian houses and the gentle River Ness flowing placidly along, but now she felt overwhelmed by the excited crowds that jammed the streets and by the color and pageantry of the games being conducted in a vast open area across from where she had parked the Austin.

The merciful numbness that had taken hold of her after the first searing pain of Ian's departure was beginning to wear off, and she looked around for some place to collect herself before she set off in search of the street where she hoped to exhibit her paintings. Getting out of the car, she discovered on the calmer outskirts of the feverish activity surrounding her a modest tea stall and gratefully sank into one of its wrought-iron chairs.

Most of the night before she had spent packing the Austin with her belongings and making certain that the croft was left without a trace of her occupancy. Then she had rested a few hours on the bare mattress in her bedroom, and as soon as she was sure the servants were up at Talbert Hall, she had gone over and given Robert the key and the *cairngorm,* in its black box.

Afterwards, she had driven off toward Inverness hardly aware of anything except that her world had been knocked off its axis and could never be put right again.

The twenty-six paintings that currently jammed the back seat of the Austin meant nothing to her now. She had stopped in Inverness only because she needed the money their sale might bring to tide her over in London until she found a job again. *If only she could avoid Alex and Avril in the meantime,* she thought, lifting her teacup to her lips.

Then—as if upon a wish—there they were, coming toward her across the grass, Avril looking cool and aloof in a white lawn dress and broad-brimmed straw hat, and Alex sporting a silver-headed cane and bowler.

"Jamie, my dear!" They descended on her like an unwelcome shower of rain.

"How delightful!" said Alex. "But where is Ian? Surely he hasn't gone off to the games without you."

"Ian couldn't come," said Jamie, and she knew at once from Avril's sharp look that the other woman had already sensed that something was wrong. She added quickly, "I've come to exhibit my paintings."

"You're down here all alone?" said Alex. "How sporting of you! Is there anything I can do to help you set up?"

There was a great deal he could do, and Jamie was reluctant to refuse his offer, but she hoped to put a quick end to the encounter. "No, thank you. I'm sure I can manage. But tell me—" She forced a smile. "What have you two been doing?"

"Having a lovely time," murmured Avril, eyeing Jamie narrowly.

"Oh, my, yes," said Alex. "We've seen everything —the long jump, the high jump, the putting of the shot. They'll be tossing the caber in a quarter of an hour. It's all very fine." He settled comfortably back in his little wrought-iron chair. "But for my money, the wrestling is the best of the lot. This morning the quarrymen took on the sheep dippers, and I wish you could have seen them go at it!"

Avril interrupted smoothly. "Why didn't Ian come?"

Jamie prayed her voice would not betray her. "He had more important things to do. Perhaps later in the week—"

"What a pity," said Alex. "We'll miss him, then. We're going down to Edinburgh on Wednesday to see Katrine."

At the mention of Katrine, Jamie felt a bolt of electricity rip through her. She hardly heard Avril's warning voice cutting in.

"Alex—!"

But Alex, once launched on a story, was never to be deterred. He turned to Jamie, his kind eyes showing a glint of annoyance. "You see, we've never met Katrine's young man, and I heartily disapprove of gaining a brother-in-law I've never so much as been introduced to."

Jamie stared at him, certain she had misunderstood. Katrine's young man? A brother-in-law?

Avril said sharply, "I would rather not discuss this now, Alex, if you don't mind."

Alex appeared not at all dismayed by her reprimand. "The cat's out of the bag, my dear. And it's high time, too. Now that I've begun, hadn't I better go on and tell the whole thing? This is Jamie, you know. You won't mind her hearing, surely." He looked back at Jamie, who was still staring at him as if she had never seen him before. "It's been quite a touchy subject, you see. If you'll pardon me, my dear, Avril has always entertained a hope that Katrine and Ian—" He cleared his throat, suddenly embarrassed. "Of course, this Gordon chap is a fine fellow, too. Or so we've been told. Cardiologist out of Glasgow. Top of his class—"

Avril said quickly, "Katrine can be rather fickle, as you know, Jamie. I thought it best not to mention the engagement until it was certain."

"Oh, it's certain, all right," said Alex grumpily. "It's been certain since the week before Easter. Found time to go to Glasgow, they did, to meet the senior Gordons, but Applecross is too out of the way, I suppose."

Avril had risen during this discourse and now she said hastily, "Everyone seems to be moving off for the caber toss, Alex."

Alex came to attention and whipped out a silver watch. "You're quite right. It's a quarter past." He got to his feet, puffing heavily. "Will you join us, Jamie?"

"No, thank you." White-faced, she gripped the table's edge. "However, I wonder if Avril will be good enough to stay behind and chat with me." Her penetrating gaze dared the other woman to move. "We have a bit of catching up to do."

"I'm sorry," said Avril, "but I'd rather Alex didn't go alone."

Alex chuckled. "Since when, my dear? But never

mind. I know the toss isn't something you're wild about, whereas a bit of gossip—" He winked at Jamie. "You'd much prefer to stay here, so why don't you? I'll fetch you in half an hour or so and we can go on then to Charles and Ann's." Giving Avril no opening to demur, he tipped his bowler and strode off with the crowd moving toward the stadium.

As soon as he was out of earshot, Jamie exclaimed, "You've known since Easter that Katrine was engaged? And you've gone on pretending that she was in love with Ian—that he was in love with her? Why?"

Avril sat down. "Keep your voice down, please!"

Most of the stall's customers had left at the same time as Alex, but Jamie complied, still too stunned to do otherwise.

"You wrote that letter, after all, didn't you? And you sent the telegram, too."

Avril's nostrils flared. She said scornfully, "Katrine's letter was six months old. I simply snipped the date off." Then fingering her collar nervously, she added with a haughty lift of her chin, "But of course I sent the telegram. If you weren't such a fool, you would have guessed that long ago."

Jamie flushed. She *had* been a fool, wondering if Ian might have sent it . . . dismissing all her distrust of Avril simply because the letter had been in Katrine's handwriting! What else had this awful woman twisted?

Her stomach knotting, she turned to Avril. "What was the point of it all?" she said, but at the same time she realized that she had always known.

Avril's venomous look confirmed it. "I certainly wasn't going to let *you* have him!"

"You're in love with him yourself," said Jamie, sickened. "You never meant to save him for Katrine. *You* wanted him!" A quick picture of Alex's kind face flashed across Jamie's brain. "Have you given any thought at all to your husband?"

Avril looked away. "He'll be glad to divorce me when he finds out I've left him."

"You called me a fool," said Jamie. "I think you're one! Alex adores you. Any woman would envy the caring he lavishes on you."

"I want a real man now!" Avril's eyes took on a defensive glint. Her ripe lips came together in a determined pout. "I want Ian—and no one is going to keep me from having him."

Rage returned some of the color to Jamie's ashen cheeks. "I'll keep you from him! Ian cares for me now. We've been seeing each other for weeks. He's given me a *cairngorm.*"

For a moment Avril was speechless, but she regained her composure quickly. "A *cairngorm?* Where is it, then? I don't see Ian, either. If there was anything of substance between you, it's over now. I knew that the instant I saw your sick, white face and heard you were alone." Gloating, Avril picked up steam. "You quarreled, didn't you? Now you've tucked tail and are headed back to London." Jamie's stricken look affirmed the assumption. "I'm right, aren't I?"

"You're evil! You've used your sister to betray your husband."

The accusation wiped the smile from Avril's face. "Don't you worry about Alex. He's had his own back from me; don't you ever think he hasn't. He's been happier married to me than he ever could have been with some frumpy, righteous dowager who would have been no fun at all. And as for Katrine—where do you think she'd be now if I hadn't looked out for her? If I hadn't married Alex? Not in a fine medical school with the wardrobe of a queen, I can tell you that. She'd be selling hosiery at Whitefish and Campbell's or dishing up tea in some tacky place like this one. Alex has poured out a fortune on Katrine. She's had everything she's ever wanted—except Ian."

Jamie sucked in her breath. "It wasn't her interest in medicine that broke them up, was it? You did!"

"Yes, I did! And why not? Why should everything go her way?"

"How *could* you? Your own sister!"

"It was as simple as straining soup," Avril answered, tight-lipped. "Plant a few seeds of distrust, and you can always count on a bountiful harvest."

A new thought struck Jamie with the force of a tidal wave. "Ian doesn't know, does he? About Katrine's engagement—"

"Do you think I'm as big a fool as you are? Of course he doesn't know." More sure of herself now that Jamie appeared so devastated, Avril preened a little. "My role as cupid gave me the perfect excuse to go on seeing Ian without upsetting Alex—before I was ready to upset him," she added hastily. "Then, of course, you came, quite conveniently, and made it so much easier. All I had to do to enjoy Ian's company was to persuade him to escort poor, lonely little Jamie to tea or dinner or a house party."

Jamie's face turned scarlet. "It wasn't quite so

convenient when you saw that he was starting to care for me, was it? You had to take drastic measures then—dig out old letters, send fake telegrams!"

Avril's smile froze, and Jamie's boldness surged. "Ian has gone to Edinburgh to see Katrine. He's there now. He'll discover you've been lying to him, and you won't get away with this."

"Won't I?" Avril's voice carried the ring of victory. "If Ian has gone to see Katrine, then it seems to me I already have gotten away with it. Katrine marries Ainsley in less than a month, and you're on your way back to London." Her sculpted lips curled in triumph. "Ian is all mine."

"He'll hate you when he knows the truth."

Avril gave her a pitying smile. "The truth can be molded. When I'm through explaining everything to Ian, it will all be someone else's fault entirely."

"If you intend to go on lying," said Jamie, "then I intend to go to Alex. I'll tell him the beautiful wife he cherishes is nothing but a cheap deceiver. What will he think of you then?"

"Go ahead," she challenged, though her voice shook. "Tell him, Jamie. Tell Alex anything you like. In a day or two Ian will come limping home from Edinburgh broken-hearted and bleeding, and guess who'll be there to bind up his wounds? If Alex objects—well, so much the better."

Chapter Twelve

With Avril's malicious revelations still ringing in her ears, Jamie pressed harder on the accelerator of the Austin as it coughed its way up the steep road rising toward Applecross. No more than five minutes had been required after their interview had ended for her to decide that she could never go to Alex. She could never be that deliberately cruel. The only course remaining was to return to Talbert Hall and see that Ian was told the truth.

Jamie had no hope of reconciliation, of course. The memory of Ian speeding off across the moor toward Edinburgh was still too vividly painful to even consider that. But neither could she ignore the ache that filled her heart each time she thought of him returning alone from seeing Katrine, all his fine hopes shattered. Her own shock at hearing of Katrine's engagement had been enormous. She could imagine the magnitude of his.

Ian had treated her shabbily. Her wounds, she feared, would never heal. But she could not forget the rapture she had found in his arms . . . the joy she had felt each time he looked on her with tenderness and yearning. He had betrayed her, but

Avril had played a large part in that betrayal, and Jamie was determined that if it were necessary for her to camp for a week on the stone steps of Talbert Hall, it would be she, not that wicked, scheming woman, who would give Ian a full account of the havoc Avril had wrought.

Nevertheless, Jamie dreaded the moment when she and Ian met, fearing that her eyes would reveal how much she still loved him, that he would hear in her voice the nuances of suppressed desire that still wracked her. Straining forward, she followed the wavering light shed by the Austin. Darkness had fallen before she reached Loch Carron, and she shivered, wondering how many more miles of treacherous road still separated her from the confrontation that loomed so alarmingly before her.

At least she could be thankful it wasn't sleeting, but even in that there was small comfort. Night had as successfully obliterated the rest of the world as the icy drizzle had done on the day of her arrival. In fact, the disadvantage this time was greater, perhaps, because the already overworked and ancient Austin carried the additional burden of her twenty-six paintings still crammed in the back seat.

Suddenly the car gave a lurch and a familiar spasm shook its laboring frame. Jamie gasped. The lights flickered. There was a sputtering noise, a wheeze, and then the engine was abruptly silent.

"Oh, *no!*" Steering as near the edge of the pavement as she could, Jamie then dropped her head to the wheel, pleading with the implacable dashboard. "Please, *please!* You have to go on!"

But simultaneously she realized what a target she was, sitting in a dark car at the edge of a traffic lane.

Was there an emergency light of some kind in the trunk? If so, would she have time to take it out and set it up before some speeding Highlander came roaring over the rise and knocked her to Kingdom Come?

She scrambled out into the road and was feverishly trying to insert the key into the trunk lid when the sound of an approaching automobile made her blood freeze. Judging from the roar echoing through the glens, Jamie knew in less than a minute it would be upon her. Then just at the moment she was sure a collision was imminent, she realized it was in the opposite lane.

The headlights fanned out over the rise. Jamie stepped across the white line in the road and flapped her arms wildly. The oncoming vehicle began screeching to a stop, its rear end finally fishtailing to within a few feet of the Austin. Moments later a dark form leaped out and darted into the glare of the headlights.

A male voice cried out, "What in the name of heaven—! Are you trying to commit suicide? Or murder?"

Jamie's heart lurched. "Ian!"

The figure froze. Then he saw who it was he had nearly run down, and he rushed forward. "Jamie! My God! What are you doing out here?"

Suddenly the wretched scene that had parted them flashed vividly in front of her, and her joyous cry of greeting died in her throat.

Ian saw her stiffen. He stopped. "What are you doing out here?" he repeated. Then his gaze swung to the stalled car, and he let out a low-pitched oath. "I told you to take the Jeep!"

Like a slap, his words renewed for Jamie the insult they had first occasioned. Her own temper flared. "The Austin and I made it fine to Inverness, thank you."

"Naturally. It was downhill. But you might have had the foresight to wonder how you'd make it back."

She drew herself up into a column of scorn. "I had no intention of coming back."

She saw his jaw tighten in the white light that bathed him. "Get off the road," he commanded. Reluctantly bowing to his wisdom, she moved a few feet onto the grass and watched as he put his shoulder to the side of the Austin and shoved it past the edge of the pavement.

"What about my things?" she called out when she saw him returning empty-handed to the Ferrari.

His answer came back harshly. "If you think I'm going to unload those damned Loch Carron sunsets out here in the middle of the night, you're sadly mistaken."

"Well, you could at least fetch my nightgown!"

"Fetch it yourself!" A door slammed, and the Ferrari's powerful motor jumped to life.

Jamie screeched. "Don't you dare go off and leave me!" Snatching her overnight case from the front seat of the Austin, she dashed across the road and scrambled in beside Ian. "Of all the rude, ungallant—"

Ian shot a fiery look across at her, but the balance of his rage went into the pressure of his foot upon the gas pedal. Jamie held onto the seat, trying in vain to recall the compassion she had felt for him earlier. Now she found herself hoping that his pain was twice as great as her own.

Once, however, as they were nearing the Hall, she thought she heard Ian sigh. Something quickened in her breast then, and she cast a guarded look at him, but he appeared as unyielding behind the wheel as a granite crag, and they finished the trip in strained silence.

Jamie had no wish to spend the night at the Hall, but she was even less inclined to ask for the loan of the Jeep to take her to the croft. Besides, she no longer had the key and the cottage was as bare as a windswept mountain ledge. With no other alternative, she trailed glumly after him into the foyer, barely able to summon a smile in response to Robert's surprised but warm welcome.

"We'll have a light supper later," Ian told Robert gruffly. "I'll ring when we're ready."

Jamie had not thought of food since morning, and she suddenly realized that part of her hollow feeling might be due to hunger. She had no idea, however, that she could get anything past the lump in her throat.

Reluctantly, she followed Ian into the oak-paneled lounge and took a seat at the game table. She folded her hands in her lap and stared determinedly at a sour-faced MacPherson ancestor glaring back at her from a gilt frame over the fireplace.

I should never have come back here, she told herself bitterly. If Ian was blind enough to go on falling for Avril's lies after his meeting with Katrine, then he deserved whatever misery she was capable of dealing him. But her eyes strayed from the dour face on the wall to Ian at the bar, pouring a glass of whiskey, and she felt such a tug at her heart that she turned away at once, tears stinging at her eyelids.

"Sherry?" he said after a moment. He set a crystal wineglass filled with the amber liquid on the table and took a seat opposite her.

He drank deeply of his own drink and then said coldly, "If you had no intention of returning here, why were you?"

Jamie winced at the harshness of his tone, but she kept her gaze steady as she countered bluntly, "Why were you coming from Talbert Hall when you were supposed to be in Edinburgh?"

Their glances locked. Finally, Ian said gruffly, "I changed my mind about going there."

Jamie sucked in her breath, every thought scattering except one. *Did he mean he hadn't seen Katrine?* "Oh, my—" she whispered.

Ian's gaze sharpened. "What is it?"

"If you haven't been to Edinburgh—" She paused, licking her lips. "Then I—then I have some bad news for you." An endless moment passed as he stared at her. "I don't know how to tell you."

"Straight out," he said impatiently. "What other way is there?"

But she saw how stiffly he had come to attention, and her stomach turned over at the thought of the devastating announcement she was about to make. "It's Katrine," she blurted out finally. "She's going to be married."

His reply came in an explosion of released breath. "Is that all?"

"All!"

"From the looks of you," he answered roughly, "I thought half of Scotland had been massacred."

Jamie stared. *Why hadn't he crumpled under the blow? Why wasn't he, as Avril had predicted, broken-hearted and bleeding?* "You're not even surprised!"

"I was when I heard it the first time," he answered curtly, "but I've had a few weeks to get used to the idea."

Her eyes opened wide. "A few weeks! But that can't be! Avril has told no one. That's why I hurried back here. I wanted to be the one to explain how it happened."

"It happened," said Ian with a brittle laugh, "because Katrine fell in love with Ainsley Gordon." Then seeming at last to assess Jamie's bewilderment, he said in a flat voice, "When I went down to Edinburgh for the Resettlement meeting that never took place, I called on Katrine. She and her fiancé had just returned from a meeting with his family in Glasgow. They thought I knew. When it became apparent that I didn't, they told me, though I should have guessed from looking at their faces."

Jamie blanched. Then a surge of anger seized her. "And you came home and took out your disillusionment on me!"

"I came home and found a jealous, prying woman eager to pick a fight with me," he retorted swiftly.

"I am not a jealous, prying woman!" Tears sprang into her violet eyes. "That's Avril you're describing. You didn't know about Katrine's engagement because she didn't want you to know. She sent that phony telegram, and worse than that, the letter she showed me from Katrine was written months ago.

She's in love with you! She broke up your romance with her sister, and she plans to marry you herself!" Jamie took a breath. "She even redecorated this house in anticipation of living here!"

Ian answered evenly, "I know all that."

"You know it!" Jamie's mouth dropped open. "And you knew Katrine was engaged to be married and you still went rushing off to be reconciled with her?"

"Reconciliation had nothing to do with my starting out for Edinburgh."

"Don't pretend that! I heard what you said when you left." Bitterly she mimicked him. "'We quarreled, we were angry, we might never have been reconciled.'"

Ian glared at her. "If you hadn't been so damned defensive, you would have realized I meant *us*. Because of Avril's disgusting trickery, you and I quarreled, you and I were angry." He came out of his chair and stood glowering over her. "You and I might never have been reconciled."

"That's a pretty story," Jamie choked. "But it won't wash. If you didn't hope to win Katrine back, why were you so furious at me for not telling you about the letter sooner? Why did you go running after her?"

"I wasn't running after her! And I was furious at Avril—not you—for her conniving. Listening to you, I realized why Katrine was so angry at me. I never got the letter she wrote me, so I never answered it. Avril handled all my mail while the redecorating was going on, and true to form, she disposed of it before I ever saw it. When you told me about it in the lane, my first thought was that Katrine should know, and I rushed off half-cocked to tell her."

For the first time his belligerence wavered. He jammed his hands in his pockets and strode across the room. From the fireplace he said, "It was a stupid thing to do. I realized that by the time I got to Dalwhinnie. Instead of going on, I talked on the telephone to Katrine and took a room for the night. Early this morning I headed back here." He turned back to her and fixed a penetrating gaze on her astonished face. "I expected you to go to Inverness with your paintings, so I watched for you on the way." Then he corrected himself. "I watched for the *Jeep*."

Jamie stared back at him. Memories of the terrible night she had spent and the miserable drive to Inverness swarmed over her. She ran her tongue over her lips. "Do you mean we passed each other on the road?"

He gave her a curt nod. "I arrived here, and you were gone. Robert gave me the key to the croft." His gaze hardened. "And the ring."

An uncomfortable silence fell between them. Jamie fidgeted with the stem of her sherry glass. Finally, she raised her eyes. "Were you terribly angry?"

His stony look swept over her. "Terribly."

"So was I." She lifted her chin. "You shouldn't have offered to buy me off with the Jeep. That was the last straw, ushering me away from here so I'd be gone when you brought your bride back."

Ian made a strangled sound. "Buy you off!"

"Well, what else was I to think? You were so hateful. You simply rode away."

"I've explained that!" he said sharply.

"You haven't explained what you said to Katrine on the telephone!"

"I'm not obliged to, you know." Then unexpectedly his tone softened. "But I will—since that was my intention when I started out tonight to look for you in Inverness."

Jamie felt a quickening sensation in her chest. She had forgotten how proud he was, how stubborn and willful—and sometimes how tender. He had set out to search for her! Her throat tightened. "Go ahead —I'm listening."

He came back to the table. "I told Katrine about not getting the letter—and about you." For a moment they stared at each other. Then Ian went on. "Of course, she was furious at Avril." His face relaxed. "But suddenly she laughed—and then we were both laughing."

"Laughing!" Jamie's shock was apparent, and strangely, Ian seemed to relish it.

"Not about you," he chided, a glint appearing in his blue eyes. "About the favor Avril had unintentionally done for us." He settled his gaze on Jamie's scarlet cheeks. "If Avril hadn't driven Katrine and me apart with her lies and indirections, we might have made the horrible mistake of marrying each other." He sat back and folded his arms. "It was a tremendous relief to realize we could be friends again."

He waited a moment and then went on, watching as Jamie moved her sherry glass in a damp circle on the tabletop. "It became apparent as Katrine and I talked what Avril's motive was."

Jamie brought her eyes up. "That she was in love with you?"

"Yes." He cleared his throat with unaccustomed self-consciousness. "This isn't the first time she's behaved so stupidly, it seems. Oh, not with me—" he said hastily and then hesitated. "Among others, with Charles Grieve."

Jamie's lips flew apart. "Charles Grieve!"

"Incredible, isn't it?" His chin jutted out. "And not very flattering, either."

Jamie could not suppress her laughter. "Charles Grieve." She shook her head in disbelief. "But why?"

"Relief from boredom, Katrine says. And a natural spitefulness. She's never been able to bear for too long anyone else's happiness."

Jamie's eyes clouded. "I think it's more than boredom this time. She was really vindictive, Ian. She vowed no one would keep her from having you."

"Then she discounted herself. Avril thrives on drama, but she always stops short of throwing Alex over. She treasures her role as Lady Stuart too much for that."

"She'd rather be mistress of Talbert Hall, I think."

Ian shook his head. "She could never bear my kind of life, even if she were given the chance to try—God forbid. All the things I enjoy, she despises." He looked at Jamie. "Can you see her helping to administer blue ointment to a sheep? In a week she'd be ready to scratch my eyes out, and she knows it. Alex, on the other hand, caters to her every whim."

"Poor Alex," said Jamie. The lump in her throat had grown larger at his mention of the day they had shared their picnic. So many happy times . . . She blinked back the tears shimmering in her eyes.

Ian stood up, suddenly restless. "Don't feel too sorry for Alex. He's actually a lucky man." He returned to the fireplace and stood with his back toward Jamie, looking down at the pots of fern growing before the grate. "I suspect he knows exactly when Avril is up to something, but nothing in the world could persuade him to give her up."

"Why not?" said Jamie, annoyed that Avril should treat so shabbily a man of Alex's loyalties.

"Because he loves Avril," Ian answered simply. "And because there is nothing so important to him as the fact that she is his wife."

The room held their silence for a moment. Then Jamie said in a voice as timid as a child's, "Ian—did you ever ask me out because Avril persuaded you to?"

He swung around. When he had recovered from his surprise, he answered gruffly, "I asked you out because I fought a battle with myself." A muscle twitched in his cheek. "I lost. You won."

Jamie's heart lurched. "Did I?" she said faintly. "You seemed to care—but then you were so cold. You stayed away from me for weeks."

"While I was waging the war," he said thickly, his eyes intent on her. "In some ways I hadn't quite healed from the wounds Katrine left, you see. And occasionally I relapsed."

Jamie got up slowly from her chair. The soft knit dress she had worn since morning clung to her slender, supple body. Shadows of fatigue rimmed her eyes, but a curious light that transfigured her face shone from them. In a voice barely above a whisper, she said, "I think you have something that belongs to me."

His proud, sensuous lips parted. "What is it?"

"My ring."

"Jamie?" Swiftly, he crossed the space between them and took her in his arms. "You can forget all of this? Wipe the slate clean?"

She nestled against him, tears of gladness streaming down her cheeks. "Can you?"

His embrace tightened, and he covered her wet face with kisses. "I would never have let you go," he muttered hoarsely. "I would have tracked you to the ends of the earth."

He took her mouth with his then, his lips moving on hers, his hands lingering over the soft curves of her body and returning to the curve of her cheek, to the tangled waves of her dark hair, to the nape of her neck.

His touch was magic, dispelling the last vestige of hurt pride and filling her with such an abundance of joy it flowed over her into her responding kiss and into the yielding of her body against his and into her hands sliding over his wide, warm shoulders.

Finally, Ian disengaged himself.

Jamie tensed, loath to let him out of her sight even for a moment. "Where are you going?"

"To fetch your ring."

He was back in minutes with the black box that had held the *cairngorm*. But when Jamie opened it, she saw on the bed of velvet not the topaz quartz, but a huge, blazing diamond resting high in a golden Tiffany setting.

"Ian!"

He slipped the magnificent ring on her finger and took her in his arms again, his eyes alight with a hot, hungry urgency.

"I meant the *cairngorm* for a betrothal ring all along, my darling, though I tried to pretend to myself for a while that I didn't. I love you far too much ever to let you go. I think I've loved you from the moment I first set eyes on you."

With glittering eyes he watched his words take effect. "But there's no time left for betrothals, my darling," he murmured hoarsely. "We need each other now—all of each other. And if the nonsense of the past twenty-four hours hasn't convinced you of that, nothing ever will."

"I don't need to be convinced." A shiver of ecstasy rippled over her, and she raised her shining face to his. "I need to be kissed."

Ian obliged her at once, and in the last moment before she lost herself in the spiraling passion of his embrace, she gave herself up to the rapturous assurance that every need of her life was met by this wonderful, willful laird of the Highlands to whom she had given her heart forever.

Silhouette Romance

IT'S YOUR OWN SPECIAL TIME

Contemporary romances for today's women.
Each month, six very special love stories will be yours
from SILHOUETTE. Look for them wherever books are sold
or order now from the coupon below.

$1.50 each

$1.75 each

Silhouette ❦ *Romance*

15-Day Free Trial Offer
6 Silhouette Romances

6 Silhouette Romances, free for 15 days! We'll send you 6 new Silhouette Romances to keep for 15 days, absolutely free! If you decide not to keep them, send them back to us. You pay nothing.

Free Home Delivery. But if you enjoy them as much as we think you will, keep them by paying the invoice enclosed with your free trial shipment. We'll pay all shipping and handling charges. You get the convenience of Home Delivery and we pay the postage and handling charge each month.

Don't miss a copy. The Silhouette Book Club is the way to make sure you'll be able to receive every new romance we publish before they're sold out. There is no minimum number of books to buy and you can cancel at any time.

This offer expires May 31, 1982

Silhouette Book Club, Dept. **SBJ** 7B
120 Brighton Road, Clifton, NJ 07012

Please send me 6 Silhouette Romances to keep for 15 days, absolutely free. I understand I am not obligated to join the Silhouette Book Club unless I decide to keep them.

NAME

ADDRESS

CITY_____STATE_____ZIP_____